LAND MINES

A NOVEL BY
SHEILAH VANCE

ELEVATOR GROUP
◦ PUBLISHING ◦

Helping People Rise Above™

www.TheElevatorGroup.com

LAND MINES

Published by
The Elevator Group
Paoli, Pennsylvania

Library of Congress Control Number 2008902879
ISBN 13: 978-0-9786854-1-6
ISBN 10: 0-9786854-1-5 Trade Paperback

Jacket and interior design by Stephanie Vance-Patience

Published in the United States by The Elevator Group.

This book was printed in the United States.

To order additional copies of this book, contact:
The Elevator Group
PO Box 207, Paoli, PA 19301
www.TheElevatorGroup.com
610-296-4966
info@TheElevatorGroup.com

PERMISSIONS

Also by Sheilah Vance:

CHASING THE 400

DEDICATION:
To anyone who is going through...
keep your head up.

ACKNOWLEDGEMENTS

I would like to thank the following friends and family who also read earlier versions of *Land Mines*: Barbara Eunice for believing in my dreams, supporting me, and traveling with me from day one with my first novel, *Chasing the 400*, as we went to book clubs, book fairs, and all kinds of events, both near and far; Stephanie Vance-Patience for the beautiful covers that she designed for *Land Mines, Chasing the 400*, and all of The Elevator Group books, and the fabulous graphic brand that she gives to The Elevator Group's works; Cheryl Hardy for working with me and encouraging me to make The Elevator Group a growing and thriving company; Connie Cannon Frazier for her friendship since our days at Howard University and for giving me the phrase "therapeutic fiction" to describe *Land Mines*; Robin Nash for those encouraging daily visits at Villanova Law School when I was writing the first drafts of *Land Mines*; Robert Vance for reading *Land Mines* with the eyes of my little brother and my attorney; Juliet Jeter for her great friendship and proofreading skills; Sherry Gressen for being the first person to read *Land Mines* and encouraging me to always honor and cherish my creative voice.

I also want to thank my children, Hope and Vance, for their unconditional love. And. I want to thank my mother, Ruth Vance Thomas, for passing on to me her strength, determination, and faith in God.

And I want to thank all of my readers. Your support is my constant affirmation.

Peace.

Sheilah Vance

PRELUDE (OR POSTLUDE, DEPENDING WHERE YOU ARE ON THE TIME LINE OF MY LIFE)

LAND MINES. I PICTURE PRINCESS DIANA, the patron saint of women in bad marriages, head and face helmeted behind indestructible Plexiglas, walking on a field, trying to find and destroy land mines before they blow up in her face or the face of some other innocent, shattering them, maiming then, changing their lives forever.

For I was like Diana, no, am like Diana. Her spirit malnourished in a bad marriage, her husband not caring whether she knew of his infidelities, flaunted them, expected her to live with them because he was a prince, the future King.

People thought of me as a princess (truth be told, some still do), living in a gilded cage, married to a man who had first power, then money. It looked perfect on the outside. The perfect couple. People were shocked when we separated. I was a good actress. But, I digress.

I cried when Diana died because she was just pulling herself together after the very public pain of leaving her marriage and getting a divorce. She seemed happy. After years, months, of sitting home alone in her castle on Saturday nights, she had found a man to love and to love her. A younger man at that. I imagine that they had great sex and that she was all over him after years of no or bad sex, except the sex that was required to produce two heirs, like I did.

She dared to leave a prince, and she died for it. Is it better to stay with the man who bores you, repulses you, destroys you, for appearances sake, for the sake of the children, or to leave, seek and find your happiness, only to have it snatched away when you are at your happiest?

Diana knew of the destruction of land mines because she had seen them in her life. She had dodged them ever since she dated Charles, ever since her mother left her and her marriage to find her happiness with another man. Diana would go along in her life, thinking that all was well, and boom, something would blow up. Taking a bit of her spirit here, a bit of her happiness there.

Just like Diana, the land mines blow up around me when I least expect it. I need a metal detector.

ﻼ

CHAPTER 1
A 'NICE GIRL' IS NOT PERFECT

2/15

THE EFFORT OF MY LIFE makes me feel like I am a salmon swimming upstream. But I don't have a home to go to. I don't know where I'm going. I just know that it feels harder than anything I've ever done because I'm not swimming alone. I'm carrying two children in my arms, and my arms ache with the effort of keeping them above water. I, on the other hand, am sinking.

I've been officially separated for two weeks. I decided it's time to keep a divorce journal and record my thoughts. Have been feeling mighty down about the whole thing. My life exposed — me, Carolyn James, a "nice girl", is not perfect. I have problems. Can't hold a man. Can't keep it all together. Can't front anymore.

Can't hide and pretend anymore. Takes too much energy and doesn't work. If I keep doing what I've been doing, I'll get what I always had. I have to open myself to more people. Be open. Be honest. Be human.

2/19

What a day! I go to work and first thing have a big meeting with the Dean about two kids in my class, one of whom's mothers is a professor at the undergraduate school and a friend of the Dean's, who I'm thinking of turning in to the honor board for collaborating on this semester's graded writing assignment, against the law school's code of conduct. A ton of bullshit later, I walk out of the room with the Dean's support and a strong desire to turn in my resignation, except now that I'm separated, I need this job. I am down for the rest of the day, saying that they don't pay me enough for this bullshit.

Just down about a lot of shit.

I have to remind myself that this separation is a good thing. I can't stand seeing Tom, the asshole I married, the father of my two wonderful children. I don't want to be around him. So many wasted years. I wonder if they will ever get better.

2/20

Today was much calmer. I had back-to-back student conferences — all from the class that I like and call my good class. Their writing may not be the best, but at least I like all of them, unlike my other class of first year law students who determine how much respect and enthusiasm they are going to give the teacher by where she is in the law school food chain, and, as a year-to-year, nontenure-track legal writing professor, I am at the bottom.

So, since I only saw kids from my good class today, I feel better, more relaxed, not crazed by it all. Conferences are over. Next week is easy.

2/21

The Women's Law Conference was great. The inner-city law school where it was held seems like a supportive environment for women. Very intellectually stimulating — unlike the plain vanilla suburban law school where I teach a low level course with a salary to match, far off the tenure track, but with health benefits for me and the kids. But, because I have to prove that I can do it all (actually, not just prove it, but do it as there is now no one I can turn to who wants to do things for me to make my life easier), I left the conference early and spent the rest of the day running around with the kids — to a store to buy presents, to two birthday parties, which I got them to late, and to the movies.

I realize I don't want to be perfect, that I can't be perfect, and that I want to be authentic. If I was just authentic, I think I'd be more relaxed — to just be me and not worry about other people's expectations. I am going to cutback on activity to find out who I am and to reclaim the pieces of myself that I gave away throughout my marriage.

2/22

Today was a definite challenge to my determination to handle all things, to keep putting one foot in front of the other without losing my mind and my spirit.

A simple trip to the grocery store turns into a three hour wait at the hospital. Indulging my nine-year-old son, David, in his post-separation sadness, the life he knew having been ripped out from under him, I tell him that he can have a donut. He takes one out of the case and climbs back into the grocery cart, the front of which I, indulgently, told him he could stand on. His eleven-year-old sister, Angela, who ought to know better, but who was playing out her own post-separation anxiety by acting out, was already inside of the cart, taunting him. As David scrambles back into the cart, he slips and hits his head on a sharp corner at the bottom of the case that holds the donuts. His head starts bleeding all over the grocery store floor, and we're off to the hospital to get stitches. Why me? Why us? What did I do? Is this normal, or just more for me to deal with? Why do I think that this is about me, and not about my son (who was basically fine, by the way, sent home with three stitches that will dissolve in ten days)?

While I sat at the hospital with guilt that will last a lifetime, Tom came because he was supposed to take David to his soccer game that afternoon, and of course I had to call him and tell him what happened. Tom was tired, nursing a cold, and was basically dispassionate about the whole thing. No feeling there. Something is really disconnected with him. I found myself saying — no way; I'm not going back to that relationship again, even if he asked me, which he hasn't so far, and which I don't think he will given all the venom and cruelty he spews my way. He's a barren, unhappy jerk who can't connect with anyone normally and with warmth. I need normalcy, passion, warmth — not him.

I left the kids with Tom and, injured son notwithstanding, I figured that I needed to have a life, so it was off to book club at Mary's. Some of the members knew that Tom and I had separated. They didn't say it, but I could tell. Either they heard it directly from Tom or they heard it from their husbands, who heard it from Tom. But some of them were unusually silent when it came to talking to me. Some couldn't even look me in the eye. But, I knew that some didn't know; they treated me the same as always. People only get uncomfortable when they know. Either way, it was an enjoyable time.

When I got back home, Tom had brought the kids back, and he was on the phone with one of the other doctors in his office, talking loud and disturbing me, as usual. I wonder why I felt that I had to deal with that for so long; why I didn't end the marriage when I realized that I was never going to be completely comfortable with him and his ways, when I realized that I had married the wrong man. Anyway, the rest of the evening was quiet and uneventful — thank God.

2/23

A great day, finally. I got some unexpected praise from students today when they learned that, starting with the next academic year, I was being promoted to become the director of a new academic advising program at the school. They burst into applause at a luncheon where some of my former colleagues were also extolling my virtues from the days when, a few years ago, I was a practicing attorney and a soldier struggling on the political battlefield with them. I didn't even know that the students cared about me. It felt great to know that they did.

.: Undated notes :.

My house (a self-help book said to write down the kind of house that you wanted; to visualize it in the mental plane until it manifests itself on the physical plane).

— Kitchen: golden brown, wooden cabinets with red and yellow accents, primary colors on the walls and accessories; very Mary Engelbreit.

— Hardwood floor; chair legs that don't need pads on the bottom of them to keep them from scratching the hardwood floors, like the ones I now have do

— Warm, golden brown, highly polished wood table

— Plenty of light streaming through the windows

— Café curtains

— An island

— Lots of counter space

House (brick? or two story informal colonial?)

— Slate walkway

— Informal flower gardens out front; lots of flowers and color all year long; a chaotic garden of color, not a perfect, highly manicured one like the one I have now

— Smaller front yard (as opposed to the acre that is now wasted and unused between the road and our front door)

— Plenty of privacy between me and my neighbors — mature trees

2/28

I am on a quest. A personal journey. I feel that I must realign my life the way that I must realign my back to be comfortable.

Maybe my back aching and feeling loose and unsupported is telling me something (a la Louise Hay in *Heal Your Life*). I feel that I need to be away from Tom's energy field and its pull to direct my own. Strange? Not according to Caroline Myss in *Why People Don't Change and How They Can*. I have to find my own lights and work with them. I feel like I no longer can be muzzled. I have to say what I have to say. Do what I have to do and not worry about the consequences. Be honest with myself and others. Why can't I tell people that I am separated? Because it doesn't come up in polite conversation? Because I don't want to talk about it? Because then they'll know that I don't have the perfect life. That it shatters my image? Who knows! I am working towards it.

Strange pains in my pelvis. Hope it's my period coming on. Have to call the doctor.

Flirted — kind of — with a guy today who didn't have a wedding ring. Felt strange, but OK. I guess I could still do it when I wanted to. Guess I still got it! But I'm not sure anymore if anyone wants it, and, if they do, how to give it away.

3/6

All of my blessings have my name on them. I can never lose what is mine by Divine right. Honesty begets what I want.

These are the affirmations I say regularly, trying to believe them. Hoping that they become a reality in my life. Grasping for anything that will make it better. It's bad, so there's something that I must be able to do to improve it. After all, for all of my life, there always has been something that I could do. If I just put forth more effort, conditions would improve. That doesn't seem to be the case now. I can put in the effort and get nothing. Or at least not get what I want, which to me might as well be nothing, because it doesn't leave me feeling satisfied. In fact, it leaves me feeling very unsettled. I hate to feel that way, but I've felt it for so long now that maybe I don't know what it's like to feel settled. Eleven years of a bad marriage with a neurotic, angry, schizo-phrenic (my judgment, not a psychiatrist's) man has definitely unsettled me.

Even my traditional anchors are disappearing. Bob, the man who I would have married 15 years ago if he wasn't married already and didn't live 3,000 miles away, the man who said he'd be my friend always, the man who said he would always be there for me, isn't. I was supposed to go to New York to see him today, but he said he was sick. I said I'll come and take care of you. He said that with diarrhea and gas, he didn't want me to see him like that. I guess he's right. But maybe the universe is right, too. Maybe it was wrong to try to see him anyway. Maybe I would have been tempted to do something that I knew I shouldn't have, like sleep with him, because I didn't like it when some other woman slept with my husband. All I know is that I am disappointed, but maybe keeping today's affirmations in mind will help. If all my blessings have my name on them, I don't have to worry about losing anything, even the soul mate-like tie that I thought we had.

I want to believe that affirmation, but I'm still disappointed that my expectation of having one wonderful day with a man who thinks I'm pretty wonderful has been shot to hell. Maybe I just won't do anything but feel sorry for myself and see what happens. I'm good at doing that. Or, I can brush myself off, go with the flow (more affirmations), and put one foot in front of the other. I'm good at that, too. Or maybe I'll just go to the Boston Flower Show and revel in God's goodness, which is nature. I need to be better at that.

இ.

CHAPTER 2
LIFE GOES ON, EVEN WHEN I DON'T FEEL SO GOOD ABOUT IT

3/7

TODAY I MADE THE RELATIONSHIP GRID that one of my many self-help books suggested. I was to list the people who have provided the most support to me in the past six months, the people who are looking for my support, and the people whose support I will need.

Then on a scale of one to ten, I had to make a support map, listing as a fraction where these people fall for me in terms of importance/strength. I find that I think that most of these people are important to me but that I get very little strength from them. I wonder if it's my failing or theirs? Probably mine since I'm the one who's looking for the strength.

Then I had to go through and think about what was the true nature of the relationship and what was needed for more balance. I came up with the following as needs: more time together, talking more, sharing more, trusting and being honest.

Then I had to think about what didn't serve the relationship. First, my old friend, the old constant in my relationship: anger. Also: preconceived notions of who I am and who I'm supposed to be; living in a shell of my life (meaning that I'm not being who I really am), letting the problems of my life (marriage/juggling family responsibilities) influence me and keep me from interacting with others; feeling a need to show perfection; me putting forth the work to maintain the relationship and them not.

I don't know where this is supposed to lead me, except to a point where I think that I have some pretty fucked-up, light, or non-existent relationships, and only a few that are very good. There's some work to do here.

3/8

I had a great day today! I started out still feeling sad and totally out of it because I couldn't go to New York to see Bob. I just felt like I was abandoned — again. But, suddenly, in the early morning hours, I felt different. The healing that I prayed for came.

I began the day calm and purposefully, the purpose being to pay bills and go through the mail. I did that methodically until Tom interrupted me with himself and the kids. He just came on in the house like he lived there. I have to stop him from coming and going as he pleases and get out from under his thumb and control. I will stop him once we get this money thing straight, because I feel very vulnerable without that being worked out, and I don't want to piss him off any more than he's naturally pissed off, although I know that he can be pissed off for any reason unrelated to me, and that sometimes there's nothing that I can do that has any effect on that.

I got my car washed too. I'm too good to be driving a raggedy, dirty and disorderly car. Very bad feng shui. I bought fabric for curtains, visited the local nursery and dreamed of how I wanted my garden to look by osmosis, not by my effort.

I finished the press release for my mothers'/children's' group activity. Hung a curtain rod. I did a lot of the things that I felt that I had to do to get on with my life. I did it all calmly, too, as opposed to the neurotic, anxious person that I sometimes have been.

I talked with Pauletta and Diane, two women who have been my friends for the past 12 years. Pauletta thinks that I can't maintain the lifestyle that I have — a 5,000 square foot house, with a $4000 a month mortgage, $10,000 a year property/school taxes, $450 a month utility bill and all of the other massive expenses needed to make it look like I can keep everything together. Who the hell is she to tell me what I can't do? Oh ye of little faith who doesn't understand me. I am having greater faith than that. I'm realizing that there's no need to be anxious... all my blessings have my name on them!

3/9

This was a very emotionally draining day. I got bad vibes at work. I was very nervous about teaching class today even though I was prepared, as usual. I got a crushing feeling of missing Bob. I wonder why? I asked God to relieve me of that feeling, that missing part. I missed a close connection with anyone I worked with, too. I felt very lonely and confused. Out of it. A phony.

Class actually went well, although I covered a lot of material in a short period of time. Instead of hanging around school, I took off early and went to the Y and got on the treadmill. I felt the need for that and to go to the grocery store. Life goes on even when I don't feel so good about it. At home, I was irritable with the kids before Tom took them for one of his visitation evenings. I just enjoyed the silence for a while.

I wallowed in my depression. I'm looking for a change. My horoscope said, "don't second guess yourself. You're ready for a change". I imagine there will be new people in my life. I'm keeping that in mind. With Bob it's either something or nothing, I think. I wonder what I'm waiting for. That's it. I am now officially fed up. I 'm not waiting anymore.

3/10

Today was much better. I felt stronger, more at ease going to work. I worked on some of the material I needed to get straight for my new job. Bob called. We had a nice conversation. He said, why don't we email, since it's hard to connect by phone. So, we'll move this into the technological age and email.

Class went well. I was calm. After class, I met a staff person on campus who went through the Master's in counseling program that I plan to start in the fall (there being free tuition for university employees, I figured that I'd get another degree. Grandmother said, "always know how to do more than one thing," and who knows whether I'll have to someday take in counseling clients to support myself and the kids). I learned a lot by talking with her.

Three of my colleagues who started teaching at the same time that I did are having problems on the job that are vastly different and worse than mine. But I can't be bothered or worried about their problems, even though they try to get me to be. Any problems they have are theirs, not mine. I'm taking my life forward. I don't have time for games, grudges, etc. Besides, they like me here at work.

∞

This is my second entry today — a two-entry day. This isn't good. That means that I'm either thinking too much or doing too much; either way, there's so much shit going on that I need to make more than one entry in my journal to understand it.

I am now bugged by this — my alleged friend, who allegedly supported me for the presidency of the non-profit organization board on which I've sat for the past six years, met with another alleged friend who also allegedly supports me and just so happens to work with my husband, and the man who is trying to jump ahead of all of us long-timers to become the board chair. These men have a secret meeting to decide my fate when they allegedly support me. Enough! I'm tired of men controlling me. I'm going to tell them exactly how I feel. I'm even more mad at the man who works with Tom because he had the nerve to check with Tom as to whether he should still even support me for the presidency. The sides are being drawn in this divorce chronicle. I'm going to call him on that, too. People said it would happen—that your so-called friends would take sides, that their loyalties would be tested and revealed. I just didn't think it would be so blatant and so soon.

I think I'll go to the meeting next week and let them all have a piece of my mind. Just because I'm going through a divorce doesn't mean that I can't think, that I can't be competent, that I still can't lead.

Or maybe I won't go to the meeting at all. Who gives a crap about them — do I need another high blood pressure-raising fight right now? I get enough of them from Tom. So, I don't think so.

And I'm not going to the going away party for the executive director of that organization, either. She thought diversity was fine in the leadership ranks until she left, then she lent her support to the old standby of corporate success — middle-aged white men. So I'm not going to her party. Who needs a hypocrite, and why be one? I don't think she did a good job, and I don't think any of them are any good.

I have to honor my feelings. They're as valid as anyone else's. I have to learn fighting strategies. Why am I even caring? I knew I didn't have the time or inclination to be chair, and I need to concentrate on my new job and change in life status. Me and my goals. Me and my career. Me and going back to school to get this Master's in counseling to plan a future for me and my kids. I feel like I'm in a rush (two years; the time before Tom can get a divorce over my objections) to really get back on my feet. I don't think I should feel that way. That's what alimony is for — rehabilitation in recognition of the sacrifices the spouse has made. I'm slowly but surely working my way back. I want to feel that I have time to do that. I am owed that, and I intend to get it, to fight for it. That's where I need to put my energies until all that is settled. With God's help, I will be strong. I know He controls all and that I have good intentions.

I also really want some love in my life. I realize how emotionally and physically empty it has been; how much I have sacrificed. The price I've paid (my soul). I'm not willing to pay that price anymore. I recognize what I need, and I am going to be open until God provides it, as I know He will.

3/11

Tom said today that he paid the mortgage and the electric and that those bills came to $5000 and that that's it. He's not paying for anything else.

I felt mad, vulnerable, a fool to have stayed all these years with this man who doesn't love me or feel a real obligation to take care of his kids, like I have to, but instead feels that his only obligation is to make more money. He makes me so mad that I don't want to even look at him.

I will take all of the mail that is addressed to him (except the bills) and leave it somewhere for him to pick up. I will tell him that I do not want him in the house. I will put all of his clothes in boxes.

I told him that his primary obligation is to support his kids. He acts like he's doing me a favor by paying the household bills when I view it as simply supporting his kids in the style to which they have become accustomed which, to them, means that they're living where they've been living; the home they've known for the past three years. I told him that is why I filed for child support and why we are going to court. I don't want to bother with him. I'm not going to let him upset me. I'm going to do what I have to do.

If he fights me, all bets are off. Just wait until the kids grow up and I tell them how I had to fight to get the money to take care of them. I can't be afraid of the outcome. The best thing I can do is to get my documentation in order and fight for what I deserve.

I'm now telling people the truth about the separation. No need to protect a man who will deny me and my children. Forget that. He's on his own. I'm not letting him control me any more. There's no need to be civil because he's not.

CHAPTER 3
WE'RE GOING TO MAKE IT

3/12

TODAY WAS SPA DAY — I did nothing but pamper myself and do what I wanted to do — slowly. Tom had the kids.

I rose at 9. Got out of bed at 9:45. Made coffee leisurely. Read my self-help stuff with coffee. Did my hair. Made an apple pancake and took time eating it. Looked at garden catalogues and ordered some stuff. Bought about 10 seed packs, on sale for 10 cents a piece, at the hardware store and some grass seed. I tried on lots of clothes when I went to the mall. I stopped doing anything when I sensed some frustration. I bought a new vacuum cleaner. I sometimes felt like my beautiful day was progressing too fast when I felt like I was taking too much time for any one thing, but then I had to remind myself — this is spa day; nothing will go wrong. I even wore my Canyon Ranch spa shirt to remind me of the wonderful time I had at that spa two years ago on spring break.

Tom brought the kids back about the same time I got home from the mall. What a surprise — the kids wanted to make dinner and desert. They picked the recipe. I found myself getting frustrated because they did things slowly and haphazardly, like kids, and then stopped myself. I snapped out of it. I didn't let them worry or rush me.

David selected chicken soup, and I helped him make that from scratch. It was delicious. Angela made a ginger cake, like light ginger bread. It also was delicious. The result was a delicious dinner that I didn't cook. I looked at their competence, their caring, and their happiness in just being together, and I thought: we're going to make it.

After dinner, I read the kids a book. Then we read a chapter in the Bible, everyone taking two to three verses. The kids practiced their band instruments.

A perfect calm day and night. I couldn't go to the spa, so I bought the spa feeling home with me. It's nice to rediscover me and to truly relax and de-stress. It's been sooooo long.

If I think negative thoughts and my mind goes racing, I remind myself to snap out of it.

Today I did nothing that I didn't want to do. That was great!

3/13

Had a great session with Dr. Williams, the psychologist/counselor that I began seeing last fall when I told Tom that I would go to counseling and do whatever I had to do to save our marriage, even if that meant drugging myself with antidepressants until the kids turned 18. After my first session with Dr. Williams, she said that, based on what I said, it sounded like Tom was the problem, not me, and in our sessions maybe we should talk about me serious-ly thinking of ending my marriage. Before I talked to her, I thought that I was crazy and that the problems in my marriage were my fault, because, of course, I figured that a good woman could keep her husband happy. I thought that it was me, and she helped me to understand that it was not.

Had dinner with my friend Rachel. It was a nice outing on the road to recovery.

3/14

Today had lunch downtown with one of my girlfriends who went through her divorce last year. Very nice. And nice to know that you can get through it and be fine, which she apparently is. They didn't have the fights about money that we have because she never gave up her career for her husband, never asked him for anything. Had I known then what I know now, which is that a man can say that he'll support you and doesn't want you to work but will pull the rug out from under you so he can freely screw some younger piece of ass, I wouldn't have given up my career. Hindsight is 20-20.

Then I went to see the movie, *As Good As It Gets* — alone. It was a great movie about flawed, closed people finding love.

I thought a lot about my love life, which is actually just my desire for a love life, because I'm not seeing anyone. Am convinced that it's as much about my need to give all the love and natural tenderness that's stored up in me as it is about my need to receive love. It will all come together one day, I'm confident.

3/16

Today was a good day. I went on a field trip with David's class to a local arboretum. It was in such a beautiful and serene setting — no close neighbors, lots of trees and nature, a mountaintop view. There I felt truly relaxed and at peace with my thoughts. Not like where I live, with neighbors too close and looking down on you from every side. I'm definitely going to buy some more trees and shrubs.

David really enjoyed having me along, too.

After the trip, I went to work for a brief minute, but I felt like I didn't belong there — not today. I don't feel close to my colleagues anymore. Also, I wasn't dressed for work and was out of the groove. Tomorrow will be better.

After fighting with Tom yesterday, I vowed that today I was going to shake off the blues and plunge into work. Just do it. Write. Practice law. Make money. Get my house and my life in order.

I mailed in my application for malpractice insurance. Tomorrow, I'll do my resume and try to get some freelancing gigs. I'm not lazy, and I'm not a punk. I can't let my troubles get the best of me. So... I came home, read one of my student's brief, cooked corned beef and cabbage, folded laundry, made sidelight curtains for the front door. No big deal (even though I had to run back out to the drug store for the thread). I just did it. I shook off the blues and just did it. I need more days like this.

It's funny; I'm going through many stages and feelings with this separation. Also, the kids haven't spent the night here for three days. That's weird, too, but peaceful. I really feel that I'm getting back, rediscovering myself after so many years of letting myself go. Sometimes I feel like I'm on a tight rope on my way back; it's a little shaky, and I see the end in sight, but it's not going to be an easy calm walk to get there. But, I love myself and know that I can and must do it.

I'm truly growing up and taking responsibility for myself. This is a path and time of self-discovery. See all the things that I can do? I feel like I'm waking up and coming out of a fog. About time.

3/18

Today was the last class for my "bad" section. I still didn't feel good when it was over. Felt like I never got through to them. They're racist, unmotivated, average, mediocre students. Why do I care? My counselor says that it stems from my need for approval.

I feel sad that I didn't get through to them after all the effort I put into my classes. Well, it's their loss, not mine, and their grades will reflect their lack of effort.

Try as I might, they didn't get all that I had to give. Truth is, they didn't want it either. Never have encountered such a group.

Then, I went to bat for some of my colleagues by trying to find them judges for their mock trials as I was finding judges for mine, only to find out that the one person on the faculty who I thought was my friend already found all of her judges and didn't tell me, nor did she try to find me any judges. That's when I realized that it's everyone for themselves around here and that was how I was going to operate. I went in my office and slammed my door. I'm tired of them. Nobody gets along. A bunch of bad and poisoned attitudes.

My horoscope said that I was in a no-win situation. Wonder when I'm going to realize it?

Then, I got home to find yet another publisher had rejected the novel I wrote last year. Sometimes it's hard to keep the faith. I'm lonely. There's no man in my life, not that I put myself out there for any to get in, but it would be nice to have some love and comfort. Then I think about the kids, who are great, but it seems like I've disappointed them, too. Anyway, the struggle continues. I'm getting it together. I'm thankful for my many blessings.

∽

I realize that my bad class made me so uncomfortable because I had outgrown that gig, because that was not the job for me. God had to make it so uncomfortable for me that I realized that I couldn't stay, had to leave, that it was not the job for me.

3/25

Today I felt as if my soul opened up. Iyanla Vanzant's essay after Day 40 in her book, *One Day My Soul Just Opened Up*, that I read today, was right on target. She said that what women needed to do was to find and depend on ourselves and God and that God would add all good things to our life. She said we'd even become so enlightened that we would interpret love songs as representing the love of God, not man. Funny, after reading that, the first song that

I heard on the radio reflected that same thought to me — that the song was not about the love and gratitude that the singer had for a man in her life, but for God in her life. God is what I need and all that I can really depend on.

When I got to work, I looked at all the self- help stuff I had put on my wall and bulletin board (to help myself, but really also to help others, I rationalized), and realized that I didn't need it anymore. It had helped me on a path, in a process, come a long way out of depression, fear, anxiety, all kinds of sad shit. I realized that the only message I needed from all of those little pieces of paper and sayings that were up there was, from Proverbs 3:5— "Trust in the Lord thy God with all thy heart and all thy mind and all thy soul. Lean not unto thine own understanding. Acknowledge him in all things, and he shall direct thy path."

That's it. That says it all. Trust, hope, love, confusion, living in the past, doubt, fear, worry. All of it comes down to one thing — trust God. He knows, and He'll do it all for you — put you on the right path. Don't worry.

I will write and expand on this later.

ऎ

4/1

APRIL FOOLS DAY. Well… yesterday I received the divorce papers that Tom filed six weeks after we separated. After 11 years of marriage. Eleven years, and he only waits six weeks to file for divorce. How stupid I felt. Eleven wasted years. Eleven years of trusting someone, doing what I thought I was supposed to do as part of the marriage thing. Eleven years of meanness.

Then, I talked with my lawyer, who recommended that I take the $5000 that he offered ($4000 for the mortgage and $1000 extra) for six months as a temporary order because even though Tom made $17,000 a month, only about $7,000 would be used to figure child and spousal support, because Tom's income stayed relatively stable at $195,000, because we're under the statutory guidelines for support, because he gets a deduction from his gross income for mandatory pension and capital contributions (a cute trick that lawyers worked out to shield money from child and spousal support), and because the guidelines would only have him give me $3,000.

"How can this be?", I ask, incredulously. True, Tom expects his income to go up so he increased the amount of money that he drew out of his practice each month, but he won't really know what his income will be until the end of the year. So, technically, she says, we can't count on that. We have to go by his income from last year. Personally, I think that he ought to look at other career options. Tom made $200,000 six years ago when he started working in that practice, and he's making less today. Who works somewhere six years and makes less money than when they started? Medicine is a crazy business.

Tom would like me to sell the house. The way I look at my attorney's proposal is that I only get six months of support for 11 years of marriage. Why do I feel like I'm being screwed? I can't move in six months! I need time to think, to save money, to find a new job. I don't want to panic or be pressured into anything, but I feel that I am.

I need to remember all of the principles today:

— Trust in the Lord; (He knows what's right).

— Lean not unto thine own understanding (because I sure can't figure this all out. What did I do wrong? Why didn't He tell me to do something, everything differently? I can't think clearly about all of this).

— Acknowledge Him in all things and He shall direct your path. (Help me! I don't know what to do. My mind is a jumble. Tell me where to put my efforts. I wrote one book; no takers yet. I'll write a second — like He's telling me.)

I know God is the source of my supply — not my husband, as Iyanla said in one of her daily affirmation books. I must remember to look to God to supply my financial needs. All things come from Him, not Tom, and there's nothing that He can't do. I need a miracle in my life, and I'm going to pray for it and wait for it.

4/5

Bad day. I need to trust more. Felt horrible yesterday and today. Worried a lot about the money. Having a pity party for myself because "no one" cares, my contribution goes unrecognized. I felt that way today, too. Out of sorts. It was Palm Sunday. I got to church late, and I left early. I didn't even get a palm. I rushed downtown to have lunch with the student that I started mentoring about six years ago. Now she's 21, and a stone survivor. Survived her mother's death from heart disease, her father's alcoholism, dropped out of high school, got a GED, and is now working in her first real job. Now she's a role model to me.

Had dinner with an old friend from college whose phone calls and emails have kept me strong throughout my thoughts of separation and these past few months. He told me that the person he knew in college wouldn't take junk off of men, wouldn't be down on herself. He said that the person he knew in college thought that she could do anything, went after what she wanted, and didn't let anyone stop her. He was right. I thanked him for reminding me of who I really was. But, we were going out, as friends, so he could comfort me. And what happened — he tried to hit on me. That was depressing. Can't I just be friends with a guy?

Anyway, I must press on.

4/6

Saw the movie *Heartburn*. Her story is like mine. Her husband cheated on her when she was pregnant, except she left him when she found out. Then she went back with him after he asked. Then he acted like everything was her fault. Acted like a jerk and treated her like one. Then she found out that he was screwing around. She put a pie in his face and left him, taking their two-year-old and a newborn. Why didn't I do that? Something dramatic?

Guess this is right.

My mother blames herself. She wonders why all of her kids' marriages are breaking up. I wonder, too. But not to worry; there's more than enough blame to go around.

4/7

Today... *"and He shall direct thy path."*

I was led to eat lunch in the faculty dining room today — the first time since January. I walked in around 1:45 (after firing off a letter to my attorney saying that I did not want to counterclaim for divorce), after most people were gone, hoping that one of my favorite faculty members, Frank, was there. He wasn't. I walked in and the top Deans were there in a heated discussion. I asked them if they wanted to be alone. They said no. They started talking to me about work, which really was the last thing that I wanted to talk about, but what could I do, being held captive by my bosses. Finally, they left. I took out my newspaper, ate, and then had a nice talk with one of the waitresses. I think she sensed my sadness. She was very nice. She gave me a free cappuccino, which was great. She said that as far as raising kids goes, don't worry, we do the best that we can. That's true.

My point — I went to the faculty dining room because I wasn't afraid anymore. After being separated for four months, I could face people. I wasn't ashamed. I didn't feel like I did anything wrong. I'm ready to put my past and everyone else's behind me. My marriage just didn't work. Get over it!

Now my Mom is feeling bad, like she did something wrong. I try to get her out of that. But it does make you think: all of us have bad marriages. I do wonder why. Guess we never had any role models of a good one. But, it's not her fault, what with our Dad dying when we were all toddlers or younger. Point — I'm shaking off the blame and shame and going back in the world. Time to re-read Marianne Williamson's *A Woman's Worth*. It's great for raising self-esteem.

5/11

Sometimes I feel like I'm in a nuthouse and I'm the only sane one.

Tom was going on and on about the money today. He said that his paying for the kid's camp fees would be like giving me a gift. No sense arguing with him or being drawn into an argument with him. He's nuts. Makes no sense. I don't understand how he or his lawyer operates. I can't believe that I'm in this position — fighting with him about money for camp or food or anything. This is exactly where I didn't want to be. Shouldn't be. All I can do at this point is trust God. But when I try to do something, it's so hard.

I get mad at the kids. Upset because the house is a mess (I just need to throw things out). I wonder if I'm obsessing. I see things slipping out of my hand when I'm trying so hard (maybe that's an answer — stop trying). I'm tired of being tired. I'm doing the best that I can. One day the kids will understand. Now, they just get mad at me, especially Angela. Some days (like today), I feel like signing the divorce papers and being done with Tom. *The Oprah Show* today was about marrying the wrong person, and people talked about how they knew at their wedding. I felt the same way at mine. Waiting to go into the church, seeing all the people inside, realizing what I was about to do, my thoughts screamed, "WHAT ARE YOU DOING? YOU DON'T EVEN KNOW THIS MAN!" (Even though we had dated for a year before getting engaged). I shook so much walking down the aisle that the minister had to tell me to calm down when I reached the altar. We had a fight about his doubts shortly after the invitations went out. I kissed up to him to show him that his doubts were wrong, but I just should have let go then, embarrassment or no embarrassment about no wedding following the wedding invitations. Because what I found myself doing throughout the marriage was kissing up to him whenever something went wrong. Oprah said to trust yourself (of course, what does she know, never having been married.)

All I can do is trust.

Actually, I can acknowledge Him by calling on Him and having Him direct my path. I'm trying to see with a single eye — like it's all good — like when I found out today that the township was giving away free compost bins and I had just thought about buying one at the local nursery for $80.

I try so hard. No one really cares — not really. I know that. Sometimes I feel like I am tilting at windmills and that I should just stop trying. Frightening to know that I've wasted eleven plus years of my life trying to be a good wife to Tom. I keep trying to be a good Mom to my kids. Mostly appreciated but sometimes thankless. I try to keep this big house together — I am going to conquer it, not the other way around.

Sometimes I feel like throwing my hands up in the air and letting the house be a mess, falling to pieces, having the yard look like shit. I just have to trust and keep on. Or, maybe I have to just walk around with my hands up, throw in the towel and surrender for minute. Sure is appealing.

5/13

I decided I wasn't going to sit here and go nuts over camp. What kind of man, a man who has money, won't pay for camp for his kids?

It came to me — write the checks, mail them, and see if he stops payment. "He will direct thy path." God telling me what to do? I hope so, because I did it. No sense in me getting angry at the kids for something that's not their fault.

I need to learn how to relax. Done!

He has $80,000 in savings; I have $4,000. The camp bill would have taken half of my savings, and I'm already staying home half days to save money on day care. No way should I feel guilty.

5/14

Victory on the camp thing. After arguments where he threatened to stop payment on the checks I wrote, he agreed. I gave him a loud talking to about providing for the kids, putting them first, not being so selfish about the money, always worrying about how it's going to affect him sometime in the future rather than what the kids need now to live stable.

Felt good all day. Tension gone from my back. "*... and He will direct thy path.*" Felt victorious. It is nice not worrying about money. It also was sunny, mid-70s, perfect. Got some time to work in the garden.

5/17

Today I'm tired, as I've been for a long time. As I do the work in the yard, the house, tending to the kids, I think — who am I kidding? Why am I trying to take care of this big house all by myself? Why do I think I can? I can't (or don't) relax because there's so much else to get done — laundry, dinner, sweeping, straightening up, weeding, pruning — I have a lot of it.

Maybe it's best for me to throw in the towel, give up the house in two years and get something smaller, although I see giving up the house as a personal failure. I guess the thought for today is — lean not unto thine own understanding — because I don't understand it at all. I try, but it doesn't seem to really work.

Same with my book. One of my friends asked me if I was going to the Boston Writers' Conference. I said no. What I didn't say was that I am so disappointed in my book not going anywhere, that I have decided not to go to anymore writers' conferences.

I was supposed to call some of my clients re: their will. Didn't. Ran out of energy. Maybe a regular job is enough for me. I should work to keep my weekends open.

Is this all there is? Is this as good as it gets? I don't know, but that's a frightening thought.

5/18

The most important thing that happened today was that, at his baseball game, David got a cycle — that's a home run, a triple, a double, and a single — and I was the third base coach. Cool! Except David didn't listen to me when I told him to play it safe and stay on base; instead, he ran and scored a run. So much for what I know. Guess I should learn to take more risks, too.

Also, Angela's game took two hours. The girls hit few of the balls, so the action was so slow that she took a break and went to the portable bathroom during the middle of the game when she was supposed to be covering third base. Boring for the girls who were playing; deadly for the parents who were watching.

⇢

5/19

TODAY TOM INFORMED ME that he was having the utilities cut off and switched to my name. What an asshole! I'm convinced — I hate him.

This evening he also was able to sit through the entire orientation program for the middle school, where Angela will go next year, and I couldn't because I had my unruly, undisciplined kids with me. That burns me up. The same day that he calls to cut off the utilities at his kids' home, he sits up there at their school like the good, concerned father — what a joke.

I blame myself for buying into the Cinderella shit/fantasy and giving up my power. The real challenge is to rise above it, not dwell on it, and move on to something positive. I guess. Tomorrow, I'm making a list of chores that the kids have to do to get their allowance. I need help around here!

5/21

Today I left for a week on an Alaska cruise. My stepfather couldn't go because he had heart surgery a few months ago. So, I filled in and went with my mother. It was nice to get away. Alaska was awesome. The women on the trip were very supportive of me. I often felt like a fish out of water, though. And sad. On a cruise with no man. How pathetic.

5/29

Tom made good on his threats. When I got back from my vacation, he had shut-off the phone in the house. I had to make frantic calls on my cell

phone to get the house phone turned back on. Then, I called all the utilities
to see when all the rest of them were getting shut off, because, how could I go
the weekend with no electricity? The electric was due to be shutoff on the
next business day. Only a complete asshole could turn off the utilities in the
house where his children resided. But I handled it. Now, all the utilities are in
my name, just as he wanted.

6/8

What a week or so. I feel good today. Have turned a corner in so many
ways.

Time to move on with my life, retake control, stop being a doormat or
feeling sorry for myself. Saw a *Montel* show on cheating. Montel told a guest
that he ended his marriage when he cheated, and how true it is that cheating
will end a marriage. Montel also criticized the women on the show for accepting cheating, for taking the men back, saying that the women had low self-
esteem and had been conditioned to believe that they didn't deserve better.

That got me thinking. Tom is a rat who destroyed his marriage, especially when I begged him not to fool around. He cheated, made choices and knew
the consequences, because I told him. And now, I have to stop feeling like I'm
guilty or have anything to be ashamed of.

On the house, my position is that Tom is paying everything for two years,
and then I'm moving to something I can afford. The rest is gravy. He's not
going to fuck with me on the money. He just had the house refinanced. That
dropped the monthly payment by $500 by not reducing the principal. And
the payment goes up 7% next year — not bad. I can live with that. Then I take
my money from him and get something else, or I get my big break and stay
here, or Prince Charming appears and I stay here. Someone better will come
along, of that, I am convinced.

Hopefully, the roller coaster is over and I can start to concentrate on my work — my job and my money-making private clients.

6/13

I get so tired of this shit that I don't even want to write about it. Writing about it means acknowledging it and giving it power.

All kinds of shit has gone on — phone cut off, electric set to be discontinued, support hearing scheduled for September! I don't understand. I've done all the "right" things or things I thought are right, and I have no clue as to why they are turning out like they are. "Lean not unto thine own understanding." One thing's for sure — I know that I don't control the outcome of a hell of a lot of shit.

I think of this house as Tom's shrine to himself and to his success. I wonder why I let him buy it. I was concerned about it, worried about it, prayed about it, and got the answer that it was ok, that God wouldn't put me in a house that we couldn't afford. Is that still true? I hope so. Otherwise, I'll feel like I was the brunt of some cruel joke.

But I also don't want to be a slave to this house. It is so big and requires a lot of upkeep. Housecleaning is my biggest expense and maybe I don't need all that, although folks with way less have cleaning ladies.

Anyway, I'm always doing some maintenance. I don't want to do that. I want to enjoy the yard, the house, the kids. I don't want to have to live up to perfection. There's no such thing. That's also too hard.

This house was Tom's dream, not really mine. Why am I working so hard to keep his dream alive? I also realized that I worked just as hard when he was here. Mainly, I did everything around this house alone. He wanted the big house, but he didn't want to do what he needed to do to maintain it.

I'd be happy with something smaller and more informal. Or, I'd be happier if I redecorated, decorated the place to suit my tastes and fixed the basement.

Will that ever happen? Sometimes I feel like a prisoner to someone else's tastes — the previous owners and Tom's. I wonder when I'm going to be able to decorate like I'd want. I'd change the kitchen wallpaper — something less "cute", less flowery, probably paint in yellows and reds. The den would be brighter, more warm, not a "man's den" with all of that dark wood and dark wallpaper. The living room would be alive and used — my room. I'm going to have to do something in there before I leave this house so that I can say for once — I really enjoyed that living room. But that will take lots of money,. Even now, I feel like God's not going to make me leave this house without my having fully lived in it. I'm going to change the wallpaper in David's room, too.

6/19

Random Thoughts...

My kids are making it with good humor and good sense while their Dad is out partying and screwing around.

— I went to my godmother's today for a church tea that was in her backyard. I noticed her massive butterfly bush — about 10 feet tall, as opposed to the slow grower, only two to three feet, that I moved from one spot to another in my backyard this year. What that tells me is to "bloom where you're planted". If I had left that bush alone, maybe it would have grown. Leave the bush alone and God will take care of it and see it grow to its full majesty. That's a metaphor for me and where I am now — I just have to trust Him.

— I'm lonely. Tom is out screwing around. He spent the night at some girl's house yesterday. He disrespects me and expects that I have to take it.

— Got with my lawyer. I told her to get me some money! It is ridiculous that he pays the mortgage but does not give me one dime for anything else for the kids or the house. She said that his lawyer says that all the money is in stocks. Don't believe it, I say. Be my advocate and check with me, I tell my lawyer, before you talk to or propose something to his lawyer. I feel like she's not doing her job.

— I resolved to be happy a few days ago. I'm trying hard. Sometimes it works. It takes as much energy to be unhappy as happy.

6/26

Had a physical fight with Tom today. He grabbed my arm and twisted it. Unbelievable to sink that low. He let himself in, took some clothes for the kids because he refuses to spend any money to have another set of clothes at his house, and a cooler. I tried to stop him from leaving with the clothes, we argued, and I lost it and smacked him in the face. He grabbed my arm and twisted it. I wanted to pick up a lamp and smack him upside the head but didn't because the kids were downstairs. He wants us to get out of the house ASAP so he can buy one. It would be great to stay and make him pay — seems fair to me.

6/27

"Make the most of what comes and the least of what goes." Great message from one of my daily affirmation books.

— All of my blessings have my name on them. So do my lessons.

6/28

Feeling better. In control. Positive, like I can do this. Think I should take the next two years and focus on my career, make money, see if I can stay in the house, take care of the kids, consider Tom a blip on the screen and keep going.

Also had my period today. No longer do I feel gripped in PMS. Have to take those anti-PMS vitamins the gynecologist recommended (B6, B 12, E) and hope that I can keep the disastrous effects of PMS at bay.

7/1

I'm accepting that this separation is about me. A quantum mind shift. About the life I want to lead, the type of relationship that I want to have. Instead of seeing myself as a victim (and hence embarrassed about it), I see myself as a woman making choices, choosing something better. I have to stop myself next time I feel pain, shame, like people are looking at me like a failure. I am a strong woman choosing a different way of life.

I felt at the start that a separation is not a divorce. I went into this thinking that we had two years to get it together, and that, until then, I didn't have to decide. That I needed time to think about things and that he did, too. I have allowed him to push me into all kinds of things too soon — fighting over money, being one. I filed for child support to get the money to maintain our home and lifestyle while we took a time out because I couldn't do it on my own and didn't trust him to do it without a court order. Tom sees leaving as exposing himself financially. He wasn't perfect, he didn't make me happy, putting up with him was not worth it, despite the material comforts, so he's angry and has to strike back at me. I feel that I can take the momentum back, take the time I need to rest, reflect, look for a better way, as I intended at the start of this separation journey. I'm going to take the break I need and not get sucked into his angry agenda. This is my agenda and my life.

7/6 — 2:30 a.m.

Feeling overwhelmed. David keeps waking up in the middle of the night, not sleeping, wanting to sleep with me, crying and disrupting things. I feel that I try so hard to keep it all together, so I ask: why me?

Maybe I will keep a gratitude journal to focus on the positive.

I reached a milestone this weekend. I overcame my holiday traveling/drive to the beach fear. Tom usually drove the two-hours when we went to CapeCod. This time, I drove down Friday morning, the 3rd, kids in tow. No trouble. We had fun on the beach all day. That night, we were wrapped in the bosom of family, my five aunts who had arrived at my aunt's beach house for the Independence Day holiday. It was fun for all of us.

Drove back Saturday. No trouble either. With Tom, it was such a hard thing to even get it together to go to the shore. I realized that much of that difficulty was my avoidance of dealing with him. My married life was pretty miserable for a long, long time.

Sunday was an easy day. Bought stuff for the kids' hamsters and a video game they'd been dying to have. I'm feeling in the money, but realizing that I have to save that money.

Feeling that life's not fair. I filed for child support to not have to fight over money! To have Tom honor his obligations. To not worry about money, and look what I got. I thought I was acting in the best interests of my children. I think that with so many decisions I make. How do I know that's true? I don't know. I guess. I just have to trust — "lean not to your own understanding" — and just keep on keeping on. Has life been this hard for women all along? When do we get to relax and enjoy?

ਕ

CHAPTER 6
TRYING TO FOCUS ON THE GOOD

7/7

BACK TO THE GRATITUDE JOURNAL. Trying to focus on the good. It's been a tough few days.

Things I am grateful for:

1) Jennifer at the cable TV company just erased the June bill rather than have Tom and I fight about who has to pay it. She's been divorced, too.

2) The letters to students inviting them to participate in the summer program went out. One less mundane thing for me to do.

3) Standing up to Tom on the "two sets of clothes for the kids' issue", meaning that I should give him another set of clothes for the kids to leave at his apartment rather than his cheap ass buying them some clothes. Even now, I'm always looking for some piece of clothing that they've left over his house, or they don't have any jeans because they're at Daddy's, or I'm washing all the time so they have something to wear, or, one of the kids has a soccer game and I realize, half an hour before, that they left their cleats at his apartment, which is half an hour away, and I don't have a key to it, which is unfair, because he still has a key to the house. Even though it's still technically half his house, I feel like he can walk in any time he wants, and I don't have the same rights.

3) My kids are healthy

4) I'm healthy.

5) My Mom's healthy.

7/10

— So maybe I'm supposed to write... sitting at home on this Friday night.

— Just found out that the only "available" guy at the law school who at all interests me, who has the best body of any of them... is gay! There goes that fantasy... and what a fantasy it was. This must be "lean not unto thine own understanding" week. Another test of my faith. To trust God, not myself because I can't even tell when someone's gay or straight. How can I be so out of touch? I'm sure there's a nice man out there somewhere for me.

Gratitude

1) I'm healthy

2) The kids are healthy

3) My mom is healthy.

4) I have enough money to pay my bills.

5) I'm in my right mind.

7/11

Today I went with Roberta to an "Adult Party" given by this group of fraternity guys who give monthly parties around town. It was a long drive to the entertainment center across the bridge in Boston, and I did the driving. What a waste. There were no appealing men. I wanted to dance but never did. Most people there were 10–20 years younger than us. This must also be "lean not unto thine own understanding." I don't understand why it was so awful. Maybe the only thing to understand was that that was not my scene, that's what.

Gratitude

1) My health

2) Got a lot of chores done today.

3) Got a manicure

4) Went out (even though I didn't enjoy it)

5) Had the money to pay my bills!

7/12

Gratitude

1) The food I bought

2) The kids returned safely from spending the weekend with Tom

3) A day to myself

4) I decluttered

5) Our house

6) Our health

7/15

Gratitude

1) My children. They are great. David said, "Can I talk to you?", and started telling me how bad he felt about so many things. I felt bad for him, but kept saying to myself, "all things work together for good" — or God — as it may be. Saw a *Today Show* segment on boys and getting them to talk. Thank God David is open with his feelings. Same for Angela. They must feel safe expressing themselves. I'm writing this sitting on his bed because he said, "Can you write with me?" We bond doing a lot of things, but he really does need others to bond with.

2) Angela's ear infection is treatable just with mineral oil drops. I don't have to run out of the house in the middle of the night (which means get them out of bed and throw them in the car because there's no one else to watch

them) to get a prescription filled.

3) I reached out to a mother I knew from the cooperative baby-sitting group we both were in when we lived in the city six years ago. I saw her in an exercise class at our local Y. We talked and shared a lot. She's dealing with a lot, too. Her husband's drug and alcohol problems and very little money.

4) I have a job.

5) I can pay my bills.

6) Everyone is relatively healthy.

7) I looked at one chapter in the second book that I'm writing and thought — boy, I can write!

7/16

1) Being able to watch David's basketball game. He shows such joy when he plays. He's an aggressive player, too.

2) I got to stay home today. Both kids were sick and didn't go to camp. My mother wasn't here to baby-sit. It was nice not to go to work because I was mentally tired, so I pruned all of the bushes in the front yard (I got sick of that overgrown look) while the kids stayed inside.

3) Despite minor illnesses, we're relatively healthy.

4) My mental state is improving. I'm not really feeling needy or thinking of myself as that, so... there's progress.

5) Angela has found something she likes to do besides watching TV — crocheting.

6) Angela started a two week diet to eliminate foods that cause migraines. We started today. It gets her to eat healthy, natural things.

7/17

More gratitude...

Two great things happened today.

1) I finally moved into my new office at work. What a change in status! It's two to three times bigger than my old one. The furniture is so nice — heavy, big and very professional. I have to keep it that way, not junk it up, live up to it. I am really grateful for the new office and the new job.

2) I cooked my first meal on the Weber gas grill. That was always Tom's domain. I guess guys think that grilling isn't really cooking, so they're happy to do that. I always thought that it was difficult to use the grill. It wasn't. I cleaned it (he never cleaned it at the end of the year), read the directions, gave it its annual checkup, threw on some hot dogs, hamburgers and veggies. I'll do more grilling now.

3) Mom arrived home safely from her cruise to the Caribbean.

4) I bought David a bike. Tom refused to. He kept trying to "fix" the misaligned wheels on the one that David had, the wheels that kept catching on the chain, jerking the bike to a complete stop and making David lurch forward. Tom would "fix" the wheels, David would happily ride it, and then 15 minutes later, the wheels were misaligned again. Tom was too cheap to spend the $100 on the bike, so I did. Typical.

5) Our health.

7/24

Today I was so sad, angry, and feeling like a fool. *"Lean not unto thine own understanding."* Merrill Lynch didn't clear the $2000 check that I sent to be deposited into my money market, trying to be a good saver. I think the check got lost. Another point of frustration. I felt like — what's the point. I try so hard, and here I am. Fucked up again.

— One of Angela's friends spent the night. The kids were getting on my nerves, running wild, up and down the steps, all over. I had to reel them in.

— Spent some time at the Y. Just looking at the folks there got on my nerves. Too many pampered women. What a contrast.

— Didn't accomplish all I wanted to at work. Sometimes I feel — why bother. I am so overwhelmed.

— One of my colleagues at work, Martin, who used to be a good and close friend, is still giving me the silent treatment. I think that he's jealous because I got promoted and he didn't. I feel that he's just a jerk. I was a good friend to him, and he wasn't the same to me. Feel unsure of myself. Maybe I'm a bad judge of character — or maybe not.

— Am reading Margaret George's *Cleopatra*. She's found a most sensuous and wonderful lover in Anthony. I wonder when I will find mine.

— Saying many prayers to God. I'm trying to hang on.

— Feeling sad because there are several people I was close to who have really let me down since the separation. When I need the people who I thought were my friends, they disappear.

7/28

Today I got major grief from Angela. She said that I need help. Need to know how to handle my anger. All because I get on her and David to be more responsible. I felt like crying. No one cares what I do, how hard I work to keep everything together around here, to not focus on myself. And for what — grief and disrespect from my kids and my erstwhile husband. Why bother? I ask myself sometimes.

This is definitely *"lean not unto thine own understanding."* I feel like a failure sometimes. Giving in sometimes. Also passed Martin in the hall at work. His hello, barely mumbled, is full of anger. I'm like, "fuck him". He's jealous that I moved up and he didn't. I was a good friend to him, and he acted like a child, and treated me like shit. And it's been about four months since I heard from my so-called good friend for the past 15 years, Bob.

Why is this happening to me? To show me that all men aren't shit? Who knows! I know and try to keep in my heart that God wants the best for me and is not out to hurt me, so I don't feel sucker punched, that I've given so much and gotten so little and wasted so much time. I wonder when I'll finally be happy in a relationship. Almost any will do (I think). Haven't had sex in seven months. Almost anything will do.

9/8

The kids went back to school today. Angela's first day at middle school. 5th grade. Tom, trying to act like the good father, comes over to help see them off.

I ask Tom to give me a ride to the Volvo dealer to pick up my seven-year-old car, which is being repaired again. I look down at my feet on the passenger's side and see this keychain with a pink flower design. Some bimbo has left her keys in Tom's car. I think — I can't go back with this immature scumbag. I can't really afford to move to a close-to-comparable house. I have to stay in the house and he has to pay for it or buy me a new house.

What a realization. He won't like it, but a fight is brewing.

Angela misses the bus home from school. Gets confused. Calls my mother and Tom because she couldn't get through to me. Both of them go up to the school to get her. How clear that Angela can't handle emergencies. She's only 11!

9/9

Big fight with Tom today. Beat up on myself for being drawn into it. I was supposed to have my birthday lunch with my two writing buddies who I met in writing class a few years ago and who have grown into such wonderful friends. But I got to the restaurant early, didn't see them, and told the maitre d' to seat me. Unbeknownst to me, they were seated on the other side of the restaurant. I sat by myself for an hour before I saw them, just as I was getting ready to leave. That fight with Tom threw my whole day off.

In counseling class, I bared my soul to the class about the divorce and today's argument with Tom. Felt good. I am myself. Others bared their soul, also.

Anyway, I think the best thing for me to do is to stay in the house. It's certainly the easiest.

9/10

New attitude today. Feel that I'll do what I have to do to make the money I need to take care of my kids — write briefs as a freelance attorney, work hard. Got some things off my desk and onto my secretary's.

Saw my counselor today. Always good. I'll hang in there and not deal with Tom unless I have to. So I get back to work, and what happens? He called. Same old same old. I'm not being drawn into these petty arguments. My birthday is in a few days. I'm going to start off my 44th year with a new attitude.

❧

CHAPTER 7
THINGS HAVE A WAY OF WORKING OUT

9/22

I'M STARTING MORNING PAGES, as Julia Cameron recommends in *The Artist's Way*. I'm getting back into writing. Maybe this will help me wake up and feel that I've got some writing done so the day is not a total waste.

This goes along with the old saying (or is it a new age saying?) — if you do what you've always done, you'll get what you've always had.

My first admissions recruiting trip for the law school is today. It would be easier if I was with Tom and could just say — pick up the kids and bring them home. I wouldn't feel so guilty about disrupting their lives. Instead, I have to work it out with my mother to be here and to watch them. I worry about and feel guilty about asking her to do this. Because of her age, which is 76. Then she acts like — always — that she can't stay at my house, for a few hours or for an evening. The kids always have to go to her house. But why can't she stay at my house? That bugs me. The point is to let the kids stay home with minimum disruption, not to run all over.

9/23

Yesterday recruiting was good. Things have a way of working out. The kids are with Tom. I had to ask him to pick them up from after-school care. I can't do it all. I worry about them and their adjustment, but they seemed happy.

I'm feeling tired, but good. I have to get my physical self together, too. I don't sleep well. I feel better about myself, though. Yesterday I got the message, ephemerally and spiritually, that some mistakes are made in private, some in public (like Bill Clinton's affair with Monica Lewinsky), and if we're lucky, we'll make them in private and learn our lessons before they're made public.

I also feel like I want love and a good boyfriend who'll be good for me and my kids. I believe that I can have the family and family life that I've always wanted for myself and my kids. I now believe that I can triumph instead of just endure.

9/25

Good morning!

What do I write today? The child support hearing is today. It's kind of anti-climactic. We'll see how it goes. On one hand, I don't get my hopes up. It seems to be just a formula.

On the other hand, maybe things will work to my favor. Depending on how it goes, I guess we'll just have to prepare to take it to the next level with a full hearing next month. I deserve to have more money. So, as my favorite gospel singer Dottie Peoples says, the battle is God's not mine, and I've done all that I can.

I'm also feeling kind of bored and empty with things. The introductory counseling class I am taking is boring, and my teacher is a smart-ass. I got right back in his world yesterday after he got smart with me. It's freeing to realize when a class is nothing, when I'm not in it for the grade, and when I know that there's no intellectual challenge there. I'll be glad to be out of his class and won't take another from him.

9/26

All sorts of thoughts going through my head.

I won at the support hearing yesterday — kind of. For six months, Tom didn't give me one dime. He only paid the mortgage (probably because it was in his self-interest because the mortgage was in his name, and if it didn't get paid it would fuck up his credit). Now, Tom has to pay the mortgage (which was all he thought he'd have to do), plus, for the next two months until the full hearing, give me $1400 a month, from which I have to pay taxes and insurance (roughly $600 a month), leaving me with $800 a month, plus, he has to pay the after-school care which is $247, meaning I have about $1000 a month to work with. Not bad. (Not great either, since the utilities, food, home maintenance and other expenses just about eat up that $1000.)

I'm proud of me and my persistence and thank God. I realize that I was right; what Tom was doing was not fair. And we'll have another hearing to see about getting more money and make it more fair.

He said (rather, his fat-ass lawyer said), he's requesting a custody hearing. The nerve of him. He'll lose that and see the kids less than before. I allowed him to spend time with the kids and now that's being held against me. Well, he can push me, but it won't work. I'll defend myself. I'm not a pushover.

Also, my stepfather picked up the kids yesterday while I was out-of-town and Mom was at Foxwoods. I resent the fact that she went gambling when I needed her. I told her that she has to help out re: my travel schedule and she acts like the hardest thing in the world for her to do is stay here at my house. Well, she has to do it a few times. I really just wish that there was one person I could lean on and who would jump in and be there for me — no questions asked — and not act like asking for help was an imposition. It's hard enough for me to ask for help, to realize that I can't do it all. I don't really ask for much, so, when I ask, I really need, and I'd like to be supported in that. I feel that if I had a father, he'd support me, and Tom would be afraid to cross him.

9/28

I feel pretty good this morning. A lot of worry has passed me by because of this hearing and knowing that I can stay in the house a while, even though I never wanted this trophy house in the first place. My endlessly aching shoulder stopped aching. Funny how that goes.

I had a nice weekend with the kids. When we are alone, it's heaven — almost. I haven't used my YMCA flex fit card, which I bought a month ago. The card gives me all the exercise classes I want for 10 weeks for $35. $35 wasted — so far. Good intentions gone bad. I'm freeing up my weekends though, coming up.

I didn't call my alleged friend Pauletta back. Why should I rush? She doesn't really care. She calls me once every three months. You would think that with all that I'm going through, she would call me more often. To me, calling is evidence of caring. I am getting so little of either from two of my old friends who I thought were some of my best friends, at least the best friends I had in this town.

Thinking of getting a hair weave with long, straight hair. Why shouldn't I look my best, too. Years of living with Tom has caused me to loose my hair.

Book club yesterday was a disorganized bomb and waste of my time. I want to talk books and literature, not socialize. Also, folks didn't arrive until 4 when we were supposed to start at three, which is when I arrived with my daughter, Angela, in tow, because David was over a friend's house, and I didn't have anyone to watch Angela. She was good, though. We were supposed to end at five, and even though we had just gotten started around that time, I left. In the old days, I would have left her home with Tom. As a single mom, I had to take her with me. There are some advantages to being married.

9/29

I didn't want to write my morning pages this morning even though Julia Cameron thinks they're so crucial to unleashing a writer's creativity. I slept poorly last night and am very tired. Real victory in last week's support hearing. My attorney called me later and said someone, somehow made a math mistake, and I got more money than I should have. But she thought that we should go with it, and that Tom would agree, according to her conversations with his fat-ass attorney. I thought — look, God has worked a miracle! Who else could work out me getting more money as a "mistake"!

God fought my battles for me. He was the lawyer in the courtroom. It all turned out fine because of Him. He fixed it and no one knew it. Now I really know — don't worry: about the book, a boyfriend, the job, anything. God will fix it! He will open doors that I can't see. He'll make a way out of no way.

This is the fulfillment of a Bible verse that I have come to lean on; one that covers all situations — *Trust in the Lord Your God in all things, and lean not unto thine own understanding; acknowledge him in all things and he will direct your path.*

10/24

Back to morning pages. I was out recruiting. Good trips to U. Va. and to the law school fair in Atlanta. Traveling was a drag, but it cleared my mind of all I've left behind. Busy schedule. I've concluded that I have to treat myself right and do nothing that will cause me anxiety. Push the anxiety away. My challenge — personally and professionally — is "me first." If I can remember that and ask myself the question, "is this good for me?", I'll be all right.

Tom had a birthday party for our son yesterday — without me. Deliberately. I'm not letting him run head games on me, so I didn't get upset, at least outwardly. I realize that I can't control everything, and that some things I just have to let go of. He had all those kids and their parents go to his apartment, which I haven't yet been in. It's a testament to how loved David is. I also found my first support check waiting for me when I arrived home. That's a testament to my persistence and determination and the fact that I wasn't a punk and didn't fall apart. I'm good at compartmentalizing so I give all the problems that I have their own time to attend to, worry about, to drive me crazy. I think I'm doing a good thing if I can think of one shitty thing at a time. One won't overwhelm me; I don't give it enough time. I have to remember to also pat myself on the back and congratulate myself for hanging in there and fighting for the money I thought I deserved and that I needed. I'm proud of me, if no one else is, because I know how far I've come and what I've overcome. God is good.

CHAPTER 8
I'VE DONE THE 'RIGHT' THING, BUT THEN LOOK WHAT HAPPENED

11/20

I AM SO TIRED OF THINGS NOT GOING RIGHT. Every time I think I can raise my head above water, an undertow comes along and either pulls me down or knocks me over if I manage to stand.

Today I went to see Tom in the hospital. He was hospitalized on an emergency basis for shortness of breath, which turned out to be a heart problem. Anyway, I was up and down the road picking up the kids. Then, this morning, my Mom said that she wanted to go to the hospital with me — like she didn't have all day to get there on her own. So I went to pick her up, and the kids and I endured her criticism–about the way I looked, the way the kids were dressed, about how I should offer to take care of Tom when he leaves the hospital because after all we're still married, about anything at all–all the way down to the hospital and all the way back. Tom was his usual reticent self — being mean to me, not introducing me to the nurses, staring into space.

On the way back home, my driver's side car window fell off its track again, leaving a few open inches at the top that I couldn't get closed. After that grueling, emotionally wrenching hospital trip, I knew I wasn't going to cook dinner. So I went to McDonald's drive through, put the window down to pay and get my food, and couldn't get the window back up again at all. Anyway, I had just paid $600 to have the window fixed. I wondered — what else! I've done the "right" thing, but then look what happened.

I wonder why things don't turn out "right". Why, when I tried to step outside the box with this divorce, I got smacked. And when I tried to stay in the box, I died. There is nothing for me to get hold of.

My next essay should be called *In Search of Happiness: Why Does It Elude Me?*

11/22

Great day today. We all got up early to prepare for Sunday school. Tom called from the hospital early in the day. He didn't have a good night. His heartbeat became irregular. He'll be in the hospital longer. Wanted to know if I was bringing the kids down. I told him about our plans for the day and said that if I was going to do it, I'd have to do it before ice skating. Showing a rare bit of compassion which I'm sure was due to his unfortunate illness, he realized that the two hours I would have spent driving them down to the hospital in the city and the skating rink in the country was a lot of driving. I had already realized that, but, putting the kids' needs first (that being the need to see their father), I would have taken them down if he said that he really wanted to see them. So I told him that I'd bring them down tomorrow.

So we went to church. The head of the Sunday school talked with the entire Sunday School — the children's and adult's classes — about giving thanks. As he said, even when everything in our lives is not going the way we'd like it to, there's always something to give thanks for. So even though I'm struggling to regain my sanity, my life and my dignity, I gave thanks for my physical health, my children, my financial support, my job, my Mom, the friends I have who do support me, and the fact that I was not in the hospital like Tom was.

In the afternoon, I took the kids to a skating rink for a party their summer camp sponsored as a way to get the parents to think the camp is run by such nice people and fork over another $500 hard-earned dollars each week next summer to keep the kids occupied. They had a great time. I sat outside the actual rink part, which was way too cold for me, on the cold benches. Two hours goes by quickly. Time seems to be flying by now, especially when I have any sort of project to finish. Everything takes longer than I think.

We had kind of an easy time when we returned from ice skating. We ate a bit, the kids played outside a bit. Today, like most days, we didn't see the neighbors. That's cool, though. Sometimes it seems like all we have to talk about is small talk, and that feels so empty when I want to talk about so much. I changed all the bed linens, finished up the wash, the kids each took a room, watched TV and read. I started dinner.

I think Tom's illness is a payback. A payback for all of the times he has treated me badly since we separated. Fighting me every step of the way about money, not giving me a dime for three months, talking to me like I was a worthless piece of shit, rather than the mother of his children who sacrificed a lot to even bring them to birth, what with one fighting with my increasingly large, painful and dangerous fibroids for room to grow, and then being born with respiratory problems (that kept her in the hospital for three agonizing weeks) while I pumped my breasts four times a day because I knew that the immunities from my breast milk were the best thing for her, going into preterm labor, and spending two months on bed rest, lying down, drugged up, only getting up to go to the bathroom, to eat, and to the doctor. Then finding out two months after the baby was born that while I was on bed rest, under doctor's orders not to have intercourse so that the baby wouldn't be born prematurely, Tom was out messing around.

They say that God doesn't like ugly, and Tom has been real ugly to me. All my new age/self-help books also say that vile people create vile diseases, so I guess what he had is payback.

Even while he's lying in the hospital, I have to take the kids to visit him and pretend that I really care about him, besides worrying about him because I don't want my kids to grow up without their father; I know how painful that is. I think about my father every day or about not having a father, even though he died about 40 years ago when I was four years old and too young to remember him or understand what having a father meant. My dead father issues continue to be substantial. How can people say that you can't miss what you never had? You idealize it, so you miss it more.

I worry that Tom will die. I also worry about myself financially. If he can't maintain his salary level, then I'm up shit's creek because I can't pay the mortgage and the other bills. Sure, if he died, I'd have insurance money, but the kids still need a father.

I had fun watching *Nick News* with the kids. They opted to forgo a bedtime story for a chance to watch the news program for kids. That was very interesting. As soon as it came on, they scrambled for a place in my bed, under my covers; I love that special time after we put on our pajamas.

I'm enjoying calm time with them. This weekend I didn't go to the law student's brunch at one of the faculty member's homes or to the book club. I realize that I can't do it all and that the kids need me and more of my time. I don't want Tom's manic behavior to affect my kids.

The car thing worked out. I went straight to the Volvo dealer and told them that they needed to give me a new car, which they did, while they fixed the broken window they supposedly fixed before. A zippy S70 Volvo that was really cool. I enjoyed driving it this weekend.

11/26

Thanksgiving was really nice. The kids were happy. We visited Tom in the hospital earlier in the day. The kids didn't even seem to miss him. They settled into the warmness of my family. Everyone stayed late watching Jumanji — even my brother. He didn't rush off, like usual, or like Tom always wanted to do. When dinner was over, Tom always waited a respectable time (5-10 minutes, it seemed like), and then he was off towards the door, pulling us along. The self-absorbed off to important matters, or so they thought.

We were tired (I know I was mentally and physically, maybe the kids too). So, we spent the night at my mother's house. We lulled away the next day watching talk shows until after 2. The kids played games and messed around, not getting dressed until around 2.

We all needed a break. And we took it. And it was great.

11/28

Every time I feel wanting, like I need something, like something's not right, the scripture, "my God will supply all of your needs" — comes to me. I'm trying to feel calm, not overwhelmed, not uncomfortable in my own house. I guess maybe I've been uncomfortable here for so long because I didn't want us to buy this house anyway (it was Tom's trophy house), that it's going to take awhile for me to become comfortable.

12/13

Great day today. Sunday School was fulfilling. I realize that Tom can go his own way. I hope he's happy. I'll be better off, and when God wants me to have a life partner and soul mate, He'll provide one. I don't have to kiss a lot of frogs, and I don't need any projects (meaning man projects).

The kids love Sunday School, God and reading the Bible. I can be around people and talk about being separated without being down about it, but accepting it as something good because all things work together for good for those that love God. The kids are resilient.

My evil mother-in-law's annual Christmas party was today. I guess Tom's old girlfriend was there, too, the source of much contention between me and both of them. I'm sure both the evil mother-in-law and the ex-girlfriend are declaring victory, now that we're divorcing. A strange group they were. I always thought that I was strange and felt out of place in their world. Now, I know it wasn't me. Their world is strange. But let them have it.

12/15

I just read I Corinthians Ch. 7 (on marriage, men and women.)

V. 15 says: *But if the unbelieving depart, let him depart. A brother or a sister is not under bondage in such cases, but God hath called us to peace.*

16. *For what knowest thou, o wife, whether thou shalt save thy husband? Or how knowest thou, o man, whether thou shalt save thy wife?*

17. *But as God hath distributed to every man, as the Lord hath called everyone, so let him walk. And so I ordain in all churches.*

I take this to mean: if he leaves, he leaves. Let him! He doesn't believe. You can't change him. God's given him a mind, a free will, a plan, and it's up to him to do what he wants, so let him walk!

As much as I can't stand Tom, I still have been tortured with thoughts as to whether this divorce/separation is a good thing, and with thoughts that divorce is not Christian or that God is punishing me with this. With all of my wondering if the divorce was the right thing, if I did something wrong, if I should be doing anything else, this scripture is a lifesaving eye-opener.

12/25

Merry Christmas! Looking back at this year, I am happy to come to this point. I am happy. I feel proud of myself with all I have accomplished. Tom came against me, and I am still here. I feel that I've turned a corner. What a year it has been, but I did it — largely against the odds. And my kids seem largely happy. One year ago, I was miserable, sensing impending doom (like the end of my marriage) with a mean, angry man. Now, I'm doing it myself — free to love and live as I please — largely. He has to support us, and I fought that fight. God is good.

❧

CHAPTER 9
I'M WONDERING WHAT'S WRONG WITH ME AND MY JUDGMENT... ?

2/21

BAD DAY YESTERDAY. Turmoil with getting my son to school with all his stuff — on time. Major mother guilt. Major wife guilt. Major bad fruit guilt.

2/26

Much better today. Thought about a lot of stuff yesterday and today. As I do in my group counseling class, I'm just going to say what I feel and screw it!

3/10

My feelings have betrayed me. Yet again. I've gotten my comeuppance. This time from Heather--another person (students are people, right?) — who I thought was a friend who knew me and my better nature, but who showed she could have cared less. I helped her and trusted her, but then she turned on me, yelled at me, pushed me away, betrayed me. I'm wondering what's wrong with me and my judgment as to who I trust.

3/12

Tom set me off again — why do I let him? Got a letter from his attorney with all kinds of threats designed to get me out of the house. Tom said that I am wasting marital assets by not selling the house in this hot real estate market and getting as much for the house as I can. He says that I am being unreasonable, that if I left that expensive-ass house that he wanted so badly and so easily left us in, I wouldn't have to ask for more child support. He's harassing me. I'm insulted and tired of his b.s. My attitude is that I'll leave that house when I'm ready, and I'm not ready. I must be strong mentally and physically, keep my head together so I can get my work done and earn a living to support my kids. I have to keep myself physically together so I can do all of the above. I wait for someone to be nice to me.

I'm going to the doctor today for low energy, finally giving in to depression. Maybe I'll have to be medically treated for it and have these pills on standby. I hate to go there. I'd rather try other means, but sometimes they don't seem like they're working. Every time I feel like I'm over a corner, Tom hits me with something else. Seems like it's taking me longer and longer to recover from the blows.

I say prayers for me and my kids. I ask God to help me.

Went swimming yesterday, which was great. Felt like a mini-spa vacation. I'll do that more often and strive to take care of myself — first. No one expects as much of me as I expect from myself. I do not want to bring on illnesses, be hospitalized, be tormented. It's "one day at a time" time and instead of thinking of all I have to do, I'll think of getting through today, with God's help and trusting that he'll take care of tomorrow. God is good, and he does have, has to have, a good plan for my life, even if I cannot see it at this point.

5/17

Pain

My pain is an indication that things aren't working.

Every time it seems that I want to rest, God pushes me and moves me on to something else through pain. Maybe I need to listen to that and just go on and be responsive to my need to change and not be afraid that I'm doing some terrible irreversible thing.

5/26

Thoughts

How can men leave their children and make things so difficult and oppressive and confining and hard for their former wives/current mothers of their children?

Maybe the answer is that men can leave their children because they don't come out of their bodies, and they don't feel it like we do. If the men realized how hard it is to be a single parent when that was not your expectation or intent, how hard it is to change your mind set when you had always planned on two, on always having someone there to raise the children together. They don't realize the tremendous mental and physical effort that formerly married mothers put forth to keep it all together. The expectations, unfulfilled and blown, weigh down. Press down on our shoulders, making it hard to put one foot in front of the other — but we do. The expectations, the guilt, the realization that it wasn't supposed to be this way, that this was not what we bought into, what we bargained for. In fact, this is exactly what we did not want because we married and then had our children when we could have done otherwise.

It's hard for us, and it spills over to our children, no matter how hard we try to contain it, to keep our fingers in the dike when it springs a leak, and finding that we eventually have to use our toes too because the leaks keep coming, and then wishing, praying that we had something else to plug the holes. Our minds are scattered, confused, wounded, hurt, disorganized and depressed — and our kids are, too. We try hard to keep the facade going; to pretend they're not as hurt as they are. Because the world they have now is not the world they have known. The world they have now is not the world they bargained for either.

We all say, "They'll adjust", and people tell us the same. But we know that adjustment is hard, and it hurts, more than we ever imagined, and it lasts until our children are grown and out of the house, off to college, 18 years. And then we can relax, breathe a sigh of relief, and know that we have done the hardest job we will ever have to do, and that only someone who has gone through it too understands how absolutely bone-weary we are, can be, and what a miracle we have pulled off. Smoke and mirrors. Magic. Prayers. Self-denial. Toughening. Cast aside.

How can men leave their children?

6/10

From Fritz Perls, now above my desk at work, "*Whenever you are feeling guilty, you are resenting something. Express the resentment and get your needs met.*" Easier said than done, especially for the single mother.

7/29

Bed-wetting

I know I want to write about bed-wetting and how my son found the cure himself. How all my pushing and pills and nose spray didn't work. How maybe we shouldn't sweat it (these developmental timetables) and allow our kids time to develop on their own and just be there for them and not rush to the next thing that we want to do.

8/7

Ways in which my life is evidenced as being out of order [making this list as instructed in the latest self-help book I'm reading]

— My kids can't find their stuff.

— My disorganization is affecting them.

— My house is infected with disorganization.

— I couldn't catch the train to one of my appointments, like I thought I could, and at the last minute, had to arrange another way to get there; I was unprepared.

— I almost missed a breakfast speaker at work yesterday because, even thought I wrote it down, I wasn't organized enough to look in my appointment book the first thing in the morning;

— I feel like crying a lot.

— I don't feel comfortable in my own home.

— my home is dirty.

— I am sad a lot.

What one step can I take to order my disorganization

— Look at my calendar first thing in the morning.

— Reduce clutter (clean up this weekend).

Daily

— Cook in advance; plan and cook meals on Sunday so there's no surprises and I have a week's worth of meals done and that's one less thing to think about every day.

— Clean the house on weekends; make our personal comfort and orderliness at home a priority; this is more than a notion; it takes time. I cannot run to or be worried about a lot of other stuff.

— Make my home a hermitage.

— Get the kids to take the dishes out of the dishwasher and put them away.

— How? Develop a schedule; go by weeks. One week per kid. One week one puts the dishes away and the other takes out the trash, and visa versa.

— Give the kids lunch money in advance. Start the week off with $25 cash per kid. Either put it away and dole it out daily, or give them the whole thing at the beginning of the week.

— Get money out of the bank weekly, every Saturday; take out $120 per week ($50 for lunch for the kids and $70 for me for everything else.)

— Grocery shop once a week; put up a grocery list somewhere permanently with a pen to write with or check off the stuff we need.

— Wash clothes once a week; every Sunday night, have everyone bring their dirty clothes down to the laundry room. I'll separate them by color, etc. I'll start washing Sunday night.

— Organize the rides needed for the week. On Sunday, look at a schedule for the week. Call around if I need to find the kids rides. (Consider buying a Palm Pilot?).

— Pay all bills twice a month only, the Saturday after payday.

(Being a single parent is no joke and time demanding. I have to make time for what has to be done without having help to back me up. There's no one but me to depend on, and my kid's health and well-being is my top priority.)

— I have to cut out some activities, cut back on some of the organizations that I feel need me or that I feel that I "have" to stay involved in.

— I need the kids around every other weekend to give them time to do what needs to be done around the house.

— I need to act, not react.

— I can do the few things that I enjoy: movies, dinner, hanging out.

— I need one of those computers with reminders.

— I need to grow up.

9/12

Today I went to the office supply store to find a calendar/organizer. I had forgotten another one of my children's doctor's appointments.

I was trying very hard to be organized, but fell short. I felt terrible — sometimes I feel like I'm losing my mind. As I work with students with Attention Deficit Disorder, I wonder if I have it. I feel that it's hard to finish anything. I run off to the next thing.

Anyway, there was a dizzying array of calendars and organizers — two rows worth. I couldn't come to terms with a size — 3 x 5, so I can carry it everywhere and write down things as they occur. But then I thought, too small. 5 x 7, I could carry it, but it'd be heavy and I'd have to get a larger pocketbook. Or 8 _ x 11 or something — desk size — so I could actually see what I'm writing down.

I found most of them lacking — too much room for appointments and not long enough to-dos. The personal organizers had a lot of room to write down non-work stuff, but then I thought — what if I lost it?

I finally found an academic (most calendars starting in the new year and this being September) weekly calendar. There was room to write appointments and to dos, but not many. Then I figured — I don't want more appointments or more to dos than would fit in a 2 x 3 inch square.

Where did it get off that we need fat, large books with lots of tabs and specialty papers. If I need that much stuff, I figure my life is too complicated, and I don't want that.

9/14

My new Book: *A Work In Progress: The Story of My Life.*

I'm beginning to think that I'm in the wrong job.

I am writing this book to help me make sense of my life. It seems like the only way I can do that is to put it on paper. I hope that my words also give comfort to others similarly situated. In the areas of work, home, personal life, things are not going as well as I think they should. I feel like I want to do something crazy — smash things, punch people. But this is much safer.

I have a job where I have to be self-motivated (but not too motivated lest someone higher up be threatened in their job). I'm supposed to help people, but sometimes it seems that I can't help myself.

I can't figure out if what I want to do is acting out or just expressing myself as a natural and logical response to things. So maybe this process will help. At home, I try to be organized and keep it together, but I don't. I forgot my son's doctor's appointment and can't get him out of the house on time and together without a lot of yelling. I try very hard to conquer these areas (be organized) and be together, but it's not working.

So, I envision this as a series of essays on things that bug me. I'm not going to write everyday. I'm going to write when the mood strikes me. With so much in my life not working (although I am thankful for God's many blessings), I think I have to make changes. Major and radical, maybe. Maybe this process will help me see what they are.

ào

9/20

I JUST READ PROVERBS 30:21-23 and stopped and paused. My Spiritual Renewal Bible said that many women compare themselves to the "wife of noble character" in Proverbs 30: 10-31 and feel sad because they don't measure up to her greatness. I think many also compare themselves to the woman in 30: 21-23 and feel sad because they are her.

21: Under three things the earth trembles, under four it cannot bear up:

22: A servant who becomes king; a fool who is full of food, an unloved woman who is married, and a maidservant who displaces her mistress.

I think of myself — and thought of myself — as an "unloved woman who is married." A married woman is supposed to be loved. But when she is not, she is sad, and the earth trembles because it knows that's not right.

How come my Bible didn't point that out and the contrast between the unloved woman in Proverbs 30 and the superwoman in Proverbs 31? I'll have to do some digging for explanations about this.

If Proverbs 30 was written by the wise man Agur back in the Bible days, it just goes to show that things haven't changed much. An unloved woman who is married can shake the foundations of the earth because she is denied so much. It wasn't right then; it's not right now.

Point, too: it happened back in the Bible days, and it is happening for all eternity. How come someone didn't let us in on that trick bag? Or tell us what to do when we are that unloved woman ... or did they?

10/13

Today as I flew back from Washington, D.C. (door to door in 12 hours, 7:15 a.m. to 7:15 p.m.), we flew right over the top of what looked like a whole field of white clouds. They looked so soft and marshmallowy — my first thought: boy, the angels must have fun playing on those. They looked like cotton balls, like cotton candy. And they were purely majestic. Not to be ignored. I tried to turn back and read some catalog full of material things, but couldn't. I had to look at the yellow light playing on white clouds, casting shadows, row after row of beauty. At times, a cloud ascended into the air like a tower.

I have a CD called *Music of the Angels*. I picked up a copy for $1.99 at the record store because I decided I needed more tranquil music in my office when folks were getting on my nerves. Anyway, on the first song, they have some light hearted harp, harpsichord, piano, bells and then what sounds like voices of kids laughing. I imagined that was how the angels laughed when they played on the cloud fields. I imagined them (and some dearly departed) hanging off the sides of the clouds, dropping down to fly, playing or not wanting to fall but having a fun game with it. At one point, the plane descended and there was a cloud wall right next to me. Another truly awesome sight that only God created.

Sometimes we need to look at the little things.

10/19

Today I bought my first stock. One week after my 13th wedding anniversary, I gave up that bad luck and did something for myself — $1000 of Martha Stewart stock. I am home today, lying in bed, trying to ward off the flu. Maybe I'm ill because I never thought I'd have a 13th anniversary and the thought of it makes me sick. Interesting. Anyway, I'm declaring financial independence and hope it works.

I bought the stock after feeling empowered by reading *It's About the Money*,

Honey, by Georgette Mosbacher, a woman who had a few divorces of her own, yet managed to end up standing and financially whole. She passed her secrets on in this book.

First, I had to figure out how to buy the stock. I called Merrill Lynch, where I'd had an account for 20 years and almost as many financial advisors because my account was never a big one that any broker wanted to keep for long, and figure that I'd make them work for my money. They got a $50 commission. I called the broker and told him what to do. He took all the information from me over the phone and bought the stock. I never even had to leave my sickbed.

Hooray!

10/20

Today was "get reimbursed for medical bills" day. Part of our settlement requires Tom to pay 80% of the kids medical bills; actually he doesn't pay it, he reimburses me, because I'm the one who makes the doctor's appointments, pays out of pocket, and then submits the reimbursement bill to him whenever I can get it together and go through the bits of doctors' and pharmacy receipts.

I get it together every time I pay my other bills and realize that I'm running out of money. So, typically, there's a few months worth of bills in what I give him. Then I have to hear him complain that I'm giving him so much at once and why don't I do it monthly? I tell him that I can't get around to it monthly because I'm doing every other damn thing to keep the kids' lives together: running them back and forth to school, to sports practice, thinking of getting the house ready for sale, looking for another one, and the list goes on.

I guess I should be happy that at least he does pay his 80%. Many women don't even get that.

10/21

Just when I think I'm going in a direction — cool, calm and copasetic — after being sick and very tired — I am brought back to my nurturing, caring role as a Mom. David still wets the bed and needs my help. He feels bad because he wets at sleep overs. How can I: write the great American novel, write a law review article, take on a freelance consulting job 10 hours a week at a local charitable foundation (which one of my well-connected friends referred me to), get promoted at work, and do this too?

I don't know. I find it hard to do more than a 9–5. I need a job that pays me well enough 9–5 to maintain a good standard of living. Maybe that's what I already have? Who knows. More thought needed. More to come.

10/26

I just read an article where some fashion designer said that people wear too much black and should change. Well, I thought about why I wear so much black, and here's my answer: I wear black because I am in mourning for my former self. For the self who expected good things.

I wonder if that's why other women wear so much black, too. Are we all in mourning for our former selves?

10/30

I am reconstructing/deconstructing my life. The life I signed on to 17 years ago when I moved back home is not working anymore. I feel pain when I attend my old church. Like a foreigner there. Like I'm a visitor, dropping in, not like someone who's been in attendance for 17 years and never really gotten involved. After all these years. Ignored. No one ever really asked me to serve in a club or organization. Wrong. Someone did once, and then she forgot about me the next year and didn't list me as a member of her group even though she listed someone who hadn't been to our church services in years, even though he never officially gave up his membership when he started attending another church a few blocks away.

The marriage I thought I wanted. The area I thought I wanted to live in. They're not working either. Not for me.

The marriage is gone, and I am adrift. Searching for a relationship that will give me comfort. I feel like the "Sister from Another Planet", borrowing on that great movie about 15 years ago, "A Brother From Another Planet", when this black guy from outer space is dropped into the inner city and has to cope. So I'm the Sister from Another Planet, surrounded by people who don't look like me. Especially at the myriad basketball and baseball games that I take the kids to. I'm always on the edge. Trying to feel comfortable. To feel at home. At ease. It seems like it doesn't have to be as hard as I'm making it.

I have to sell my house and buy another. Deconstructing/reconstructing the physical place in which I live.

But what about the mental? Nothing feels right anymore. Nothing fits. Relationships come and go. Deconstructing/reconstructing. Looking for comfort.

Maybe it is time to move on. To somewhere. To change scenery. To take a break. To have that nervous breakdown that I've been pushing away for so long. Maybe then people would leave me alone. Would realize that I'm tired. That I need space. That I need help. That my life is not working, without me screaming it out every chance I can get.

But they can see that it's not working. Some of them. The observant ones. The others say, "You look good." They don't know. They don't look beyond the surface. They don't want to know.

11/3

What is it about Chinese food and single women?

I stopped by my local Chinese takeout to buy dinner (just came back late from a three-day road trip for work and decided to charge my dinner to the school, which I just learned I could do if I came home late enough, rather than try to find something at home to heat up). I placed my order and went to the grocery store while I waited. By ordering takeout and not being a martyr and doing everything myself, including cooking, and by using my expense account the way I guess it's supposed to be used, rather than saving the school money and denying myself, I felt like I was doing something for me. I finally realized that I was worth it. I came back to the restaurant and a pretty blond, 30-40ish woman was sitting on a bench in the entry way, waiting for her order. She yawned like I did, too. I wondered about her — why is she here, alone, in this neighborhood, when her "look", the pretty blond, is so highly prized.. If she can't find a man out here, where most of the men (I'm assuming) want someone who looks like her, what hope is there for me, a regular colored girl with short hair hidden underneath a long hair weave, a once slim 5'4" body now approaching average weight with the girth that's starting to form around my abdomen, dark circles under the eyes from too little uninterrupted sleep?

Then, as I picked up my food, another single woman, more plain looking but also tired-looking, picked up her food. Dinner for one. It was Wed. night. We were all alone, but at least we were eating good.

11/30

Writing about writing or a work in progress. Life. What of it? I write because I have to. To find joy. To keep from going crazy. To let the thoughts in my head out instead of staying in and crowding each other, ready to explode.

∴ Undated again ∴

Sports athletes as role models

Trying to set an example for my son, I watched ESPN with him rather than going into another room and lying down, tired as I was. A football player from Stanford won the ESPN award for best athlete. First, he gave honor to God for blessing him. While waiting for the next award to be presented, the network reported on another football player who got in an accident when, driving with his girlfriend, the tires on his Mercedes blew out, and the car spun around. He said as soon as it happened he called out, "Jesus", and he knew that he'd be OK. Then they announced the 1999 Heisman winner, and as soon as he got up, he said, "first giving honor to God" for blessing him with his talents.

My son said, "is that what I should say?" I said "Yes, Praise God."

12/15

We had to give our seven-month old Lab mix dog, Tippy, back because of my daughter's allergies. That was a blessing in disguise. I was tired of taking care of that dog. It was like having another baby — feed it, teach it how to toilet itself, put it in its pen (crib), let it out for some exercise, etc. A mixed blessing. But the dog was just starting to make some real progress in some areas.

At least I didn't look like the bad guy in this situation. When the allergist told me I had to get rid of the dog, I made the kids come into the examining room and hear it from him. They know that I thought that I could make it work. It is hilarious that I thought that I could buy that huge air cleaner to take enough of the dander out of the air to make it not be a hazard for

Angela's asthma. I also thought that Labs didn't shed that much hair. Well, maybe Labs don't, but Labs mixed with who-knows-what do shed. And they shed a lot.

I got us a dog out of guilt. Major mother guilt. The kids kept badgering me about getting a dog. First I resisted because of the allergies and the asthma and my desire to not make either of them worse. Then I thought I could handle that part with the air cleaner. Then I resisted because I never thought the time was right for a dog. But then I asked myself — is there ever a good time for anything? How do we know when things will turn out right? I thought it was a good time for me to get married, and look what happened. Is there ever a good time for a divorce?

I knew that dogs took time, and I just didn't want to do it. But then divorce guilt hit. Big time. The fact that I had ruined/was ruining my kids' life was bad enough. The least I could do is get them a dog to provide them a little comfort in this trying, desperate, depressing time. So I gave in.

12/19

My brother came and picked up the dog today. She'll have a good home with him and the kids. Run of the house. Lots of love and a yard to run in.

I'll miss the dog, but, really, it was like having a baby and so tiring. I think the kids feel that too, but they'll never admit it. Anyway, I wonder if it would have been easier if I had a man around the house to help.

                              ᵌ▲

CHAPTER 11
YOU ARE NOW ENTERING THE TWILIGHT ZONE

> **WARNING DEAR READER:**
>
> *You are now entering the Twilight Zone (January to June 2000)*

FOR SIX MONTHS, I didn't make any diary entries. A six month chunk of my life is missing. Gone. Vanished. Never happened. Or at least never recorded.

I knew there was a period when I was so overwhelmed, frightened and disgusted with myself that I didn't want to write, lest the act of writing it down would make my life all the more real, something that actually existed, in black and white, not easy to forget, which is what I wanted to do with a lot of my life then.

I couldn't believe that my life then was my reality. Writing it down made it undeniably mine, but I wanted to pretend that it didn't exist because so much of it wasn't turning out as I had hoped. And, the effort of my life was much harder than I ever imagined.

As I look back to reconstruct my life for six months, some very significant things occurred. I decided that the new millennium not only signaled the changing of the centuries, it also signaled that it was time for me to date.

So, on January 1, I declared that I was ready to start dating. Two years without a man in my life and two years with no sex was long enough. Then on January 8, I met Carl when I was in New York at a conference. He was about 13 years older which, initially, attracted me to him because I always wanted an older man, figuring that he'd have more sense, be more mature, more willing to consider me his trophy, and, hence, more willing to treat me kindly. I was wrong, but I digress.

We had a few dates, but something about him always bothered me. Maybe it was the fact that he'd been divorced for over 20 years and had never remarried. I figured that any decent, educated man with a good income, which he said he had, wouldn't last that long on the open market. And then I got the feeling that I was out with my grandfather, although my grandfather would be about 100 years old now. It's just that I don't really consider myself to be as old as I am, and people are always telling me that I don't look it. Also, it wasn't that at 59 his age was so old, because I have a friend who is that age who seems as young to me at 59 as he did at 43 when I first met him. It was that this 59-year-old was old-acting. His mannerisms. His hair. His wrinkles. He could kiss his ass off, but I wondered if I could ever make love to him with what I figured was his wrinkly body, if his neck and face and hands were any indication of the rest of him. It sounds cruel, and it is, but I'm being honest.

So I let the relationship drift away. Then I got involved with Allen, who was 16 years younger than me. We were on the board of the same non-prof-it group, and when he started flirting with me at the Christmas party, I had to straight out ask him if he was flirting with me because it felt like that, but I figured that I must be wrong. I wasn't. What I also really wanted to ask him, but didn't, was, "Do you know how old I am?", because if he knew the answer, I was convinced he would go away. But, when he found out the answer, he didn't flinch.

After a few false start dates where we got our signals crossed and my hopes dashed, we finally went out. And we ended up at his apartment. And we had sex. And it was so great that I wanted to cry. But I didn't. Instead, I eager-ly said yes later that evening and early the next morning when he reached for me again.

And I felt that after my two-year hiatus, I still had it, and, heaven knows, a young boy still wanted it. So, for a good two to three months, I reveled in his flat stomach, long "you know what," and kisses that made me wet. But it was so good to me that I wanted it all of the time, or more often than I got it, or, I just thought that since we enjoyed each other's company and loved having sex together, that we would get together often. Isn't that the way it's supposed to be? But I thought wrong.

Yes, he enjoyed my company, enjoyed having sex with me, but didn't want to plan ahead as to when we would get together because he never knew when he'd have to be working and he didn't want to disappoint me by planning ahead. Of course, all of that could have been rectified if we just made the damn plans and then, if he couldn't make it, he called and told me so. I'm a big girl. I can take that.

But no. . . he has to end it. One day, we go out for dinner and a movie, first time in a few weeks. He brings me home and tells me that he's leaving. That's it. No sex. Of course, I should have known that something was up when I was in my bathrobe, waiting to get dressed, clearly naked underneath, when he picked me up, and he didn't jump me right then and there. I thought — OK, I bought into that stereotype, that men were looking for sex first, anything else later, and I checked myself for thinking that sex was the first thing on his mind. I shouldn't have doubted it, because if a man has an opportunity to get a shot in before doing the other, non-sexual things that he has to do to keep a woman happy, he'll get the shot in.

Anyway, he tells me that he's leaving that night and, not straight out, but basically, that he's not coming back. I sink so low as to essentially beg him to make love to me one last time, and he refuses.

So I start beating myself over the head, replaying the tapes, wondering what I did wrong to make him leave and running a real guilt/shame trip on myself by thinking how could I ever have been so dumb as to think that a fine-ass man 16 years younger than me could take me seriously — a needy, scared, and recently separated middle-aged woman with two pre-teen-aged children.

I know I didn't write because I was so hurt and so shocked and so think-ing that it would be a good long while before I ever find a good man, and why couldn't I have been one of the lucky few who finds Mr. Right — or at least a great boyfriend — the first time out.

But I also think that I didn't write in my journal for the past six months because I was so busy writing academic shit for my professional survival that the last thing I wanted to do when I got home was to write, not to mention that I was thoroughly exhausted. As the economic realities of divorce became clearer, I realized that I was in a position where I didn't want to be — I need-ed that job. That job that was supposed to last only for a year until my first novel became a best-seller and gave me the money I needed to leave my bad marriage. But it didn't. So I held on, sure in the belief that I needed a job with benefits in my own name. That was true, but now, with child support uncer-tain and alimony certain to end, I had to hang on.

The coin of the realm in academia, the path to a brighter, more secure future and financial growth, is scholarly writing and presenting papers at con-ferences. So, I set about to do that with a vengeance. I presented at every major conference in my field, a total of three, and wrote law review articles for two of them. My first presentation was in January at the annual law schools' conference. I worked on that paper from July of the previous year up until January, when I presented it. Then I wrote and researched for months on draft after draft until I turned in the final draft in May.

Then I had to present at another conference in August. This time I had a co-presenter, and we decided to turn the presentation into an article since we did so much damn work on the presentation that it really wouldn't take all that much more work to turn it into an article. Wrong. In my opinion, it took a lot more work, mainly writing and research, but I did it.

And, in between those two presentations, I was on a panel at a third conference in May. I didn't have to write a paper, but I did have to research before I presented. On top of that, I took two writing classes over the six month period because I wanted to better hone my skills. Each week we had a writing assignment, which I found myself working on at home because there was no free time at work.

So, basically, I was tired of writing. Plus, that was not a time in my life that I really wanted to record for all times sake. It was a time I wanted to forget.

Tom was badgering me pretty hard about everything — money, when I was going to sell that big ass house that I never wanted and get him out from under that mortgage that he said he could afford, why I wouldn't let him spend more time with the kids (answer: because I wanted to lessen the impact of his crazy, schizophrenic angry ass on them, and because I was convinced that he wanted to spend more time with them because he wanted to cut down on the child support he paid, Massachusetts having just moved to a proportional reduction system — the more time the kids spent with the noncustodial parent, the less money the custodial parent got. And I was tired from always fighting him, always being criticized, always being treated disrespectfully and disregarded.)

And I was afraid. Afraid that I had made a mistake by not trying harder to keep the marriage together, although I don't know what any rational person would call two bouts of counseling sessions with two different counselors, and my totally giving up of myself to please him and keep my family together, if that was not trying. But, I was afraid that I made a mistake in not trying even harder to keep us together when it was he who really made the decision to end it by leaving, he who couldn't wait to be free to screw his little yoga instructor/ bitch/slut/whore whenever he wanted to.

But I was afraid that I was going to fall on my face. That I'd never find the love I always wanted. That no man would ever really love me. That I wouldn't get the money to buy a new house. That I'd be struggling financially and have to turn the children over to him. That my book would never be pub-lished, and my dream of being an author would fade. That I was being a bad mother and setting a bad example. That I would never be happy because I didn't want to write all that down, to face all that, to honor that as my reality — who would?

So, I didn't write. But I picked it back up again when the relationship with my young lover fell apart, and I didn't know how else to express the ter-rible, fearful feelings that I was having except to write them down. I've always been much better at expressing myself in writing than orally. So, when I was so hurt that I didn't know what to say or to do, I turned back to my refuge, my life-long source of comfort: my journal, my friend.

ða

CHAPTER 12
STEP BACK AND LIGHTEN UP

6/2

THIS IS A JOURNAL ENTRY THAT IS really a letter to a man I don't feel that I can talk to; in and of itself, that's a problem. One of my books said that if you can't say it in person, say it in writing. So here goes:

⌒

Dear Allen,

I am scared and hurt because you don't call. I feel like you don't care for me or about me. I feel that if you really cared about me and wanted to know me, I would be in your head and on your heart and you would call. I don't feel special when you don't call. I feel anxious, thinking that you are slipping away and that I must do something (call you) to keep you close. It feels one-sided, not like there's equal need and caring and sharing. I have so much I want to share and talk about. I feel like you should want to call me and talk about it all. I feel stifled, even though you're not here. I feel that there are certain things that I can't tell you because you don't care enough to call me about them or anything else for that matter.

I need you to call me, not just say that I can call you anytime I want to talk. I miss you, and I'd like to think that you miss me. My life can be so complicated, full of duties and decisions. I'd like to share it with someone. Maybe that's one thing this weekend has shown me. In the course of caring for my children, I would like companionship to support me and brighten my way. I don't want my children to be a chore. I need a man to support and love me.

Maybe you don't call because... a million excuses and reasons. But they all come down to one bottom line... you don't call because you don't care.

I also realize that, even if I have the kids, I have to arrange for a babysitter to go out and meet my needs. Life goes on, even with kids.

I worry that sex dominates our relationship. Worry may not be the word, concerned might. It's not worry because the sex is wonderful and caring and when we're together, I get a sense that you do care, so much.

I guess what I really want to do is drop my anxiety and tension and fear that I will be found out and hurt from caring for you too much to really build a friendship, a relationship, having you as a man I can depend on, rely on, enjoy, be with, and trust.

I guess this is a stage, a phase. I really don't want to be hurt. I really want to open up and be honest. I want to tell you my needs and have you meet them. Instead of having a conversation as to why don't you call and your answer being for me to call you, maybe I should say that I also want you to call me because that will ease a lot of my fears and make me feel special.

Somehow, I don't believe it when you say that I can call you. Is it that I don't believe that I feel comfortable enough with you to trust what you say? Either way, I don't like this feeling, and I have to do something about it. We have to talk. I guess I have to let you get to know the real me, or just get to know me, my down side as well as my light, my thoughts, my feelings. Because what I want from you is to share all of that and more, including going places with you and having you as my lover for as long as I am making love with anyone, which I hope is a long, long time.

That's a lot to cover. I think that I can see now that I've masked my feelings. I really want it all at once. And I think that if I don't get it all at once, the relationship will end. I have to realize that I can take it easy, can work my way into things, that God directs my path and steps and yours, too. That rushing any of it is a sign of a lack of faith in the future. There's a process going on here that I'm not quite sure I understand but need to flow with.

No more relationship books, I think. I don't want to listen to people tell me what I should and shouldn't do. I want to listen to my heart and my God and pray for relief from anxiety and fear and to keep my head in love and on love and to trust the process and the timing. As Lady T (Tina Marie, one of my favorite singers) said so well, "God will do the gifting, all we have to do is wait." And pray. And ask God to move in my life to bring about a right resolution of my love life. To ask him to direct my path. To fill me with happiness, peace, joy and contentment and trust the process that leads to that. And move away from people and thoughts that aren't like that. To be still and know that He is God. To practice what I believe in.

To slow down. To do some things differently. To seek pleasure and contentment. To enjoy and be prayerful. To take it to God and leave it there. To be light, to be love, to be peace, to be joy, to know — "all things work together for good for those that love God." To allow him to work in my life. To shed sadness, discontent, anxiety, fear, etc. To be fully actualized. To love my neighbor and to be in love and charity with him and her. To realize that I can have it all. As God has provided for others, He will do for me. A good husband and a happy home. To realize that there's no scarcity of love and support and accept all that comes my way.

Operating out of fear is not good. If I'm operating out of fear, that's my operative motive, then I need to back up, check that feeling and do something else. Pray and stay in his presence and trust Him.

Realization Release. Resolve. Yet another affirmation.

6/4

God's will for me is happiness, and HE delivers the blessings.

I would like to be blessed with Allen's love, but only God can deliver that. I have done all that I can do. All I can do is wait. If that is a blessing God has for me, if that is within His will as part of/a plan for my happiness, then God will deliver that. I have done all I can do at this point. I must be at peace and be still.

6/5

Dear Allen,

The solution to my inability to talk to you is to write it down here. Like some high schooler or grade schooler who has a crush on a guy and is afraid to talk to him and she writes in her diary. Except I'm not afraid to talk, not really. You just don't want to hear my talk. I am trying to give you the space that you want, but it's not so easy for me to turn off the desire to talk with you when I've been doing it for the past five months.

I thought of a solution to your fear of disappointing me by not seeing or talking to me as much as I want. I'll just go back to dating someone else besides you. Then I won't be sitting around waiting for you.

I talked and shared with you because you said you wanted me to and because it was the right thing to do. I'm trying not to second guess myself. I was honest... blah, blah, blah! I'm not going to get into this self-pitying, rehashing this stuff again and again, ad infinitum. If something occurs to me to tell you, instead of doing mind torture on myself, I'll write it here. That's all.

I hope you feel the love I have for you, the good wishes I hope come your way, the affection I have for you. That's real. It hurts and makes me sad not to express it, but I hope by writing this, you feel the love I'm sending your way. Take care.

Love, Me

6/6

9:30 p.m.

Dear Allen,

Me again. Here's what I think I need to do and am going to do — step back and lighten up. I think that will be the key to your problems and mine. We ought to just have fun together, whenever, w/o expectations because some fun is better than no fun. That doesn't mean my feelings for you have changed, because they haven't. It means that the way I interact with you will change — at your request. I think that will be good for you and for me, too.

Maybe we had too much, too soon, and the weight of it was crushing you and me. I think that's true. So, maybe this is a good thing. The reconfiguring of our relationship so that it is better for all concerned and all around. All things do work together for good for those that love God, even if we can't see it at the time.

6/7

There's so much I want to say to Allen, but I'm not sure that I will remember it all on the phone with him, even though I've had the conversation with him in my head a million times. So, I'm going to write out what I want to say to him so I don't forget or get paralyzed the moment I hear his deep, tremulous voice. So, all of the things I want to say are...

"I'm glad you said what you said and did what you did. So much of what you said was right. I needed to step back and lighten up."

"I got a revelation."

"I'm sorry I made you feel bad, pressured, anxious, conflicted." (Although I really think that he should be apologizing to me.)

"I definitely don't want you to feel pressured to call me, see me or make love with me."

"I'll never repeat that scene." (The one where I lost all dignity and begged him to stay, to make love, after he took me out to dinner, led me on, let me think that we'd be making love because we did every other time we were together, knowing I hadn't been with anyone else and wanted him so, leaving me high and dry.)

"My feelings for you are unchanged, but I believe I need to change the way I interact with you." (Even though it's by chance, not choice.)

"I always love to see you, but it's not fair for me to try to fit you into my timetable and then be anxious about it when you don't do things in my time."

"I think we need to lighten things up — I only want to enjoy your company, have fun with you, be your friend."

"I will back off my interaction with you and leave the ball in your court. I'd love to spend time with and enjoy you while you're here, and even if and when you get another job and move, but only if you truly want to."

"Don't feel that you have to do anything on my account or that I'll feel hurt or angry or bad if you don't."

"I still am sending you nothing but love and I will continue to do that."

6/8

Dear Allen,

I don't understand. We talked.

You said you wanted the love I had in my heart for you. But you don't call.

You said that you hoped there wouldn't be less interaction with you when I said I was going to change the way I interacted with you. And you still don't call.

I said it wasn't fair to try to fit you into my timetable. That I read all kinds of things into that when you can't do things with me when I am free. And here is one of the first tests of whether I can overcome that — my class tonight. You know that I have my class. You know I'm free, but you don't call or come like you have on so many Tuesdays in the past five months. So many times when I looked forward to the end of class and you coming over my house, making love to me, making my week.

I am trying to not read anything into that. To believe that you do want me to love you. Why am I doubting that? Because you're staying away from me, as part of your process, I guess.

You acted happy to see me today when I dropped by your office after my board meeting, but it's clear that you weren't following up for more. That's when I said I would leave it — not brooch the issue. Put the ball in your court and wait for you to make the next move.

But it's hard to do that. Maybe it means that I don't trust you and I have more work to do on myself. I'm trying to keep my focus on me. I think that will hurt less.

Let me send out love and good things to you and figure out why I'm still anxious.

I miss you. Old habits do die hard.

—   **Me**

11:27 p.m.

CHAPTER 13
STOP CHASING THE HAMSTER

6/10

TODAY I TOOK MYSELF TO THE BEACH. Allen didn't want to go with me. He said in that light, but now annoyingly mocking voice, "rain check, rain check". Carol first said that she'd go but then bailed out because her boyfriend's crisis was more important than mine, although she was very helpful in clarifying where I was in my relationship with Allen — essentially nowhere. My sister-in-law and her kids didn't want to go. So I left home about 10:30 and came home at 8. A great day. Mostly stayed on the beach, slept and walked to the boardwalk. The day was a triumph for me, for my independence, for my reentry into the world. I love the beach, but what I loved most about the day was that I did it myself. I made it happen. I decided I wanted something, and I just did it. Me. An independent woman.

6/10

I'm keeping a gratitude journal, just like every other unhappy woman in America who has listened to Oprah or read *Simple Abundance*.

I am thankful for:

1) Taking myself to the beach alone when no one else wanted to go

2) Driving down and back safely

3) My health

4) My family

5) My mind.

6/13

The loneliness I feel is like a hole in my stomach, a hole that can't be filled. I miss Allen so much. I ask God for help all the time. I'm not exactly sure what to do. I seek support from my friends. Ask them what to do, and still come up confused. Please help me God. I don't want to be in pain.

6/22

Back to writing again as an alternative to talking.

Dear Allen,

I'm afraid of you now. Afraid to say what's on my mind for fear of scaring you off. Afraid to ask you to do something for fear that you'll think I'm pressuring you. Stuck. Words choked in my throat — unable to get out. A body that craves you, but yet you deny me. So what am I supposed to do with my feelings? With the love that I have to give, which you said you want. But you only want it your way and in your time, and our ways and times aren't clicking.

From you I'm feeling snatches of the meanness and control that I felt when I was married. I never want that again in a relationship. I'm thinking that maybe this relationship isn't working for me. I certainly don't like how it feels. I feel pushed away. Ignored. No mutuality.

I wonder if you're coming to my party on Saturday, and I shouldn't be wondering. Ramona's right — if you care about me, you should be offering to help me with the party. So far, you haven't. You've just made fun of the whole idea — calling it a garden party. Predicting that twenty people will come when I said I sent invitations to 70. Why would I want to be in a relationship with someone when he doesn't try to help me, ridicules me, etc. This is my self-loathing, masochism rearing its ugly head.

I don't know what to think about where we are. I think, maybe, I'm taking it all so seriously because I've forgotten what it's like to date. I've been married for the past 11 years. I desperately want this relationship to work. I'm scared, and I so enjoy making love to you. In fact, I can't imagine a better lover, and Lord knows I want that.

I'm just really perplexed. Maybe you'll pick up that vibe. I'm sending out love to you, but I also need love from you. I need to feel it. To see it. To experience it. I am going to pull back and stay back until you pull me out, until I feel like it's safe to come out. Otherwise, I'm putting myself back on the shelf. I'm sorry about that. I miss you, but I'm also afraid now.

6/23

Enough about Allen. He was a self-indulgent flirtation. Time to get serious.

The child support wars. Preparation for the next hearing.

Notes to my attorney:

— File for more child support and alimony pendente lite if you are sure that I will get more money. My income as of 6/16 is $61,000.

If my income is such that it moves this support battle outside of the statutory guidelines (because I get screwed by being locked into the statutory formula, which doesn't give me enough money to pay for this big-ass house he bought and left me in), then fine. If not and if allowed, add the $5500 I receive for a summer research grant to my income figure. If adding that in moves my case outside of the guidelines, tell me what I have to do now to prepare for the hearing.

— Also, should my desire to increase monthly support be part of the negotiation surrounding the July hearing? If so, is the more prudent course not to file for the increase and use that as part of the negotiation? Let me know your thinking on this.

I do not want to file for more money now if it's going to screw up my chances of getting a good resolution out of the hearing next month. I would rather wait until after that if you think that's the right thing to do. Pls. let me know ASAP.

Also, before the hearing, I assume that we will need to meet again to talk about exactly what I want and assure that we're both on the same page.

— Miscellaneous musings:

— He borrowed against his pension for $25,000 to buy his BMW. Why can't he borrow to pay me the money that I am due?

— Also options for me to get a down payment — a home equity loan on the house, paid off when the house sells — aren't there any other options that you know of?

All of the above: a desperate cry in the wilderness to my attorney to help me get more money and make sense of the senseless.

6/24

Another self-help book has led me to ask and answer this question:

What old patterns do I want to release from my life?

— Fear, dependence, hate, anger, low self-esteem, indecision, extreme contemplation, loneliness, boredom

What have I been missing? What do I need more of?

— Love, fun, sex, happiness, peace, joy, hilarity, companionship

Is there a dream I've been wanting to realize?

— A happy marriage; writing a blockbuster novel

What do I need to do to make dreams a reality?

— Write. Find a good man.

(Both easier said than done)

6/26

The answers to more self-help questions. I'm not writing down the questions, just the answers.

The nature of my disappointment.

1) The specific incident or occasion that precipitated my pain was Allen not agreeing to see me when I was free. It was painful every time this happened. And him not wanting to have sex with me the last time I saw him.

2) My pain is related to unexpected occurrences because I thought things were going well in the relationship and in my life generally. I thought that after all the hard work on myself, all the time I put in on myself, with myself, that I was getting the reward I wanted and deserved — a loving relationship that really came out of nowhere. And I was ready to put myself back into it — or that. I didn't really see it coming. I thought he was more serious and desirous of seeing me. I thought he wanted to see me as much as I wanted to see him, but I was wrong. And the fact that I was so wrong and misjudged him makes me scared and puts me off balance. I thought I knew better, but I didn't. I guess this shows me that I have a lot more work to do on my perceptions. But that I also can't control him or anybody. But I feel that if I can't rely on my perceptions, what do I have? Maybe this is just showing me that I have more growing to do. My love life hasn't been a crystal stair, and I guess it won't be.

3) My concern is for myself and that's where my pain comes from.

4) Yes, I believe it came about because of some shortcoming on my part. If I was more perfect and wonderful, of course he'd want to be with me. The fact that he doesn't makes it about me, not him. Of course, maybe my poor self esteem is showing, but maybe not.

5) Yes. My idea about myself, how the world works, about others and my relationship to the Divine has been impacted. I used to think that I was

desirable, that I was a good judge of character, that I had come to the point, after long dark nights, where I could relax in and into a relationship with Allen. I believed that I was finally getting my reward and showing that there are good men and relationships out there.

Now I believe that I'm not quite as desirable as I thought. I believe that I misjudged the situation with Allen. That I'm back to that safe people thing again. I think people are one way; then I look and see that they're another way when they blind side me and hurt me. I am afraid now and going back into my shell. I don't believe I have come to the point where I can relax in a relationship with Allen. I was wrong. I don't believe there's really a lot here to relax into, despite what he says. I kind of believe, as Malcolm X said, that I've been hoodwinked, bamboozled, etc.

My relationship with others — I used to believe that Allen wanted a relationship with me. I used to believe that he really liked me and wanted to spend as much free time with me as possible. I used to believe what he said about how he felt. I now believe that he is not as wild about me as I thought. I now believe that he's pulling back and pushing me away. I now believe that he's more selfish, self-centered and controlling and manipulative than I ever thought possible. I now believe that he has a mean streak in him. That he believes in perfection. That he doesn't truly love and care for me. That in some ways, he's playing with me. That there's a bit of cruelty there — opening me up to him physically, then shutting me down.

I believe that I can't really trust him, that I have to walk on eggshells around him, that he's not as enamored of me as I thought, and that — God forbid — he may be seeing or interested in someone else, especially since we haven't made love in 5-6 weeks and I don't think men go that long without it.

My relationship to the Divine has been impacted. I used to think that God was all kind and loving and blessing me with the good things that I deserved and have worked so hard for. I used to think that God thought that

I was worthy of having these good things in my life. I now think that God is not giving me his best — sorry God. Your best to me is what I prayed for — a good man who would love me and my children. It seemed like you revealed Allen as the unexpected answer to my prayer six months ago. You have allowed me to get close to him, to have him in my heart, then you go around and take him away, shake things up. Everything felt so good and right and now it feels wrong. Now you're pulling him back, withdrawing, denying me the things I once had, sex being a lovely manifestation of that, companionship and affection another. I wonder why?

I've wondered often whether this is/was some cruel joke. And I wonder whether I'm being punished and/or what I did wrong. Then I stop and think and know that you're not trying to hurt me. You're trying to help me. I get my faith back. That you are a good God who wants the best for me and that although I can't see it now, this is for the best. And that all I can do is trust you and keep on keeping on, living my life, putting one foot in front of the other, praying, trusting.

But I believe you're also telling me to lay back, stay cool, give him a chance to come back, as you told me one desperate night — you're proud of me and how I've kept my faith and ability and put one foot in front of the other and worked through things and how great I am and how I should just "love yourself and let others love you." It's hard to just lay back and do nothing, but maybe this is the lesson I need to learn now about relationships. To love myself and let others love me. Or, as Sabrina says, to stop chasing the hamster and let the hamster come out on its own.

6) The disappointment doesn't impact my means of survival, but it does my role/identity as a girlfriend and one who is worthy of having a loving relationship in her life.

7) My biggest concerns about the situation are — it will end, I will be alone, I won't find a better lover so I'd better stick with this one, I'll be lonely; it's over.

8) Good question (whatever it was). I don't feel that I can trust myself to make a realistic assessment of the severity of the situation. I question my judgment. I don't feel that I am the greatest judge of other people, especially men. I am in turmoil about so much. This equitable distribution thing, fighting with my soon-to-be-ex. I have been out of the dating world for so long, my instincts about the whole thing, how it works, etc. are shaky. I don't really remember how I approached it 14 years ago. Because I'm always open to growth and because my life is going through so much change, I'm not sure whether this is just another change I'm supposed to go through. I really can't trust myself. My perspective is distorted by fears of the future. You can call them unsupported, but I don't know how unsupported they are.

I probably am oversimplifying and over generalizing this.

9) The anger and fear I am feeling probably is not being expressed to a degree appropriate to the objective threat or impact. I think I am making more out of it than it is — because to listen to and believe Allen, it's nothing bad, it's all good. Even if it's something bad, I can pick up the pieces and go home and go on. It really is not like it's the end of the world. Life will go on. If God wants me to have a good man, He'll send me someone else. If Allen is the good man for me now, He'll work it out. God will provide. God will do the gifting and all I have to do is wait, says Tina Marie, who I sure would like to see in concert next Saturday, so please God have someone ask me out for that because I've bought so many concert tickets over the past two months that I'm not buying anymore right now.

10) What hasn't been impacted by this situation? Not much because it had such an impact on me, it has impacted every other area of my life, because I'm in every other area of my life.

11) Similar situations in the past have been resolved by my retreating back

into my shell, staying away from that person, either hoping that he'll come back but basically realizing that there's other men out there, that I can't make anyone want to be with me, that it's his loss because I'm great, by going on with my life and putting myself back out there for others. I've never really stayed in my shell. I might have been confused and withdrawn for a while, but I always come back out. This thing hurts and I want to remove hurt from my life. So either we get it together so it works for me, or I put it behind me.

This time is different because I don't think I have that many options or chances for a good or better relationship. It's not like men are standing in line, waiting to date me, and none that, as of yet, give me a real rush. This time is different because I'm not used to getting hurt. I had so much invested in this. He's so young and great, and it's the first real dating relationship of any consequence since my separation. That may be one reason why I'm so nuts about it.

It's hard. It's new. It means a lot more. Maybe realizing and remembering that is the key to put it in perspective — he's not the only good man out there! I am great enough to attract other good men. Just give myself time, lighten up for sure, and step back and see what happens. Take the pressure off of him and me. Enjoy my life. Enjoy other people. Stop sitting around and being depressed. Keep busy. Do some things differently. Finish my work so I can move on to other things. Work at home in a more comfortable, comforting, nurturing, loving environment, but get out and do the things that I enjoy.

12) I'm not sure that I have the emotional, spiritual, mental and physical resources necessary to bring about the resolution I seek. I need more strength, ability to concentrate, ability to focus my mind, ability to put the past behind me. I need more faith, trust. I need more fun and kindness thrown in my direction. I need more peace and equilibrium. I think

I have sufficient information. I need to use it more wisely. I need to forgive myself.

13) For any discrepancy, I accept the situation. There's no outside help to seek, except my friends' loving and supportive ears sometime. I continue with my counseling and will bring it up there.

14) I do feel stuck, but I feel that I can get moving. I have to lighten up and not pin all my hopes and dreams and happiness, present and future on this one relationship. I need to put that last sentence in bold, neon lights somewhere.

I am just going to go on and live my life and be happy. If Allen wants to come along for the ride, great; it would be great for both of us — I think — if we'd both just relax and enjoy. Otherwise, I have a lot to give and to share and somewhere, some great guy will want what I have to give and he will give me all that he has to give. So rather than running from, being frightened by love or the problems I am currently experiencing with love, I should immerse myself in love and loving thoughts, radiate love — even if there's not an object for that love — and let it come to me. I will be love, loving, sexy and have the calm, peaceful, joyful mind set of a loving, sexy woman in love. If the *I Ching* is right, then when the effects produced are right, all those who are receptive to the vibrations of such a spirit (love) will then be influenced and come to me of their own free will.

❧

CHAPTER 14
HOW COULD I HAVE BEEN SUCH A FOOL?

6/28

Dear Allen,

Still writing after all this time — incredibly. I am hurt and hurting. I am writing because I refuse to call you. I can't believe you didn't come to my party, my "garden party" as you called it. Thirty of my friends came, but you didn't. Could you care for me so little? Basically, I can't believe what's going on. How you're treating me. I don't like, but what can I do about it. Pray for strength to hold my ground and move on. I can't make you come to me. If you want to come, you'll come, and I assume you'll come better than before. But I think the best thing for me is to forget you. Just like I did with Tom. If you really want me, if there really is something here, you won't let it die. If you do, there's nothing here. I've tried to see you; I've called you. You haven't reciprocated, and it hurts to even write this.

How could I have been such a fool? A bad judge of character. Stupid. It doesn't matter the reason — the results are the same. I'm alone. No one cares for me the way I want to be cared for. Bottom line. I hope to get it one day. Some of the happiness that I have long been denied. Please help me God. I ask for help all the time.

Anyway, I still wish you'd call. I guess I'll be making real progress when I no longer wish that. But for now, I do.

Sometimes I wish that I would grow up and have the health, happy relationship that a mature woman should have. Hasn't happened yet.

6/28

Dear Allen,

Two letters in one day. A record! Anyway, I wonder if this is a relationship we should work on. I keep thinking about you, hoping that you'd call but not knowing what to say. On my path of self-discovery, I read all these things about hanging in there and working through difficult times, working out conflict instead of walking away, as I am normally inclined to do. I wonder if I should do something.

But then I think maybe I'll do the wrong thing, so I do nothing. But that may be the right thing to do. Just nothing. Just wait. A lot of times I think the relationship is over. That you don't want me in your life (but then I think maybe you just don't want me in it now) and that you're not interested in being in mine.

But, then, I think, maybe this is just me giving and/or you taking the space you need, slowing things down. Darned if I know, so my inclination is to do nothing and see what happens. To be with myself. To force myself to focus on me and do what I need to do — whatever that is!

7/12

Dear Allen,

Boy do I miss you. I've thought a million times about picking up the phone and calling. But I don't want to put myself in the position to be rejected again. I'd like to arrange to see you, but deep down I know that if you really want to see me, you'll arrange that.

I want to close this relationship if that's where things are. To my way of thinking, that's where they are. You asked for space and time, and you've had so much of both. I wonder if you're seeing someone else. I guess the answer's yes. I would be seeing someone else if any of the guys who said they'd like to date me would follow through. I'm trying to move on, but I'm not able to — the people aren't there. I wonder if I cling to you in the hopes that there's something still there because you called last week. I don't know. I wonder if you have another lover. At first, I ached for you. Now I've turned that part of me back off again. I can't even remember, or should I say, I block out thoughts of what it was like to make love to you.

In many ways, I'm pitiful, and I'm sick of myself. I want help. I need help. I want to be cared for. I want to be happy. For so many years, I was unhappy in my marriage... and blah, blah, blah! Who cares? I'm sick and tired of being sick and tired.

Anyway, I hope you're doing well. I hope you catch the vibes I'm throwing at you. I think that all I can do is wait. I'm not in control of this — I've tried that and failed miserably. I'll give up the controls to you and just step back and wait and see if you pick them up and drive on with me.

♣

CHAPTER 15
MY PRE-BIRTHDAY PAMPERING SEQUENCE

7/26

I JUST READ ANOTHER SELF-HELP BOOK, *All the Joy You Can Stand* by Debrena Jackson-Gandy, and it talks about pampering yourself and taking care of yourself first, because others will treat you the way that you treat yourself, and if you aren't happy with yourself, you can't be happy with another person, and if you aren't worth pampering yourself, no one else will do it. So, I'm in. I've accepted the fact that I don't have a boyfriend. It is just about 40 days before my birthday. I am going to begin a 40 day, pre-birthday pampering thing, vowing to do one good thing for myself each day, vowing to treat myself the way I want others to treat me, vowing to be better when I turn 45 (which suddenly seems so old to me) than I was the year before.

My Pre-Birthday Pampering Sequence

7/27

Today I took an hour nap when the kids and I got home. I was exhausted, jet lagged and feeling the effects of the sleeping pills I've been taking because I needed a few nights of good, uninterrupted sleep to keep it together. I took a nice bubble bath after dinner and had an ice cream cone. Then treated myself to a beautiful, visually appealing, appropriate movie — *How Stella Got Her Groove Back*. Fun.

My soon-to-be-ex, me, my lawyer and his fat-ass lawyer had a 4-way meeting, and a financial settlement that was favorable to me was the result. So I treated myself to some happiness, too.

After my bath, I laid on my bed naked and wrapped in a towel and let myself air dry. I am thankful for my two good kids, my healthy Mom, my health, coffee with Allen on Tuesday because I'm trying the "even though we can't be lovers, we can still be friends" thing.

7/28

Not a whole lot today. Much of the day was spent packing for my trip to the Virgin Islands — another gift to myself. But — I treated myself to 20 minutes of Tai Chi with the tape that I bought weeks ago but haven't had time or didn't make the time to use.

God is good.

I also treated myself and the kids and two of their friends to the *Nutty Professor 2*, although the movie wasn't much of a treat for me. Too much sex, sexual innuendo, cursing and bathroom jokes. PG-13 — not good for kids 10 and 12.

7/29

Pampering

Took a bath and lit two candles. Watched *Sex and the City* instead of working on the draft of my law review article. Figured that I could do that tomorrow, when I'm fresh. Rubbed my lovely mango ambrosia lotion on me and smell great.

Gratitude

1) That the kids got to camp safely and are away for two weeks.

2) That they're good kids

3) That Karen drove the kids down to camp, saving me from driving my car, which I don't feel 100% comfortable with because, even though the dealership fixed the fuel/engine/turbo problems on my 9-year old car, I don't

know when the next thing will go wrong because something goes wrong so often.

4) That Sabrina called just as I was sinking into feeling bad that Allen hadn't called and followed up on all the major things going on in my life the last few days. I guess I'm not going to expect him to call. I pray that I can just go on and live and not even hope in the smallest recesses of my mind that he will call me. I look for total surrender.

My mantra (thanks to Iyanla):

Today I surrender, I release, I detach from every person, every circumstance, every condition, and every situation that no longer serves a divine purpose in my life.

...that says it all!

7/30

Pampering

1) Rented the movies — *End of the Affair* — a love story — and one of my favorite cheer me up movies — *To Wong Foo Thanks for Everything Julie Newmar* — a story about loving yourself, being your flamboyant self, not worrying what others think about you, yet still spreading love. I even watched some of it before I started on the law review article, which I had to have ready tomorrow.

Gratitude

— Today I got $200,000 in my divorce settlement (even though almost all of it goes straight into a pension account, and I can't touch it until I retire). Surprise! I basically agreed to a divorce today. We had the settlement conference before the judge on everything we agreed to last week in the four-way meeting. Even though I had practiced family law, I didn't realize that the attorney's intent was to have the hearing officer grant the divorce on the day of the settlement conference. The conference, which was really like a hearing because it took place in some mini-room that looked like a courtroom, went faster than I thought. That's it. Over and done. I'm divorced. Just waiting for the signed, sealed and delivered decree. I can't fight it. Everything is done in divine order.

I guess it's time to move on, but at least I'm moving on with more money than I ever thought I'd get.

8/1

Today I pampered myself by going in to the city and hanging out with some friends who were in town for a national convention. First, I went to a reception that was given by one of my old clients, then I went to a continuation of the reception at this huge hall where I met my old friend George Harper, then to the Black History museum, where I ran into Donald Henderson, who is this guy I met earlier this year in New York. Then George and Donald and I went back to Donald's hotel, the Grand Marquis, and had drinks in the lobby. It was fun talking to both of them. Donald and I met at the dance in New York where I went with Carl, but wasn't really wild about going or about him, but my girlfriend said, go; you might meet someone else. How right she was.

I also was dressed really nicely. Today was a "Say something hat day," which Patrick Swayze declared in a wonderful scene in my now favorite cheer-me-up movie, *To Wong Fo*. On a "say something hat day", you dress up really fine, forget about your troubles and what other people think of you, and go out there looking your best in spite of them. I really had fun.

Gratitude

1) My spirit coming back

2) Running into George

3) Running into Donald

4) My Mom

5) My health

8/2

1) Took a bubble bath

2) Took a nap

3) Went out with Donald to convention events even though I left home at 11 p.m. — stepping out of my comfort zone, because I usually don't go anywhere at 11 p.m. except to bed.

8/3

Pampering

1) Met Sabrina for coffee at Barnes & Noble to give her an overdue birthday present even though I had a ton of work to do

2) Bought myself two bathing suits and a cover up even though I was initially concerned they would be $80 and I shouldn't spend that much on me, but I did, and it turns out that they were on sale and only came to $51.

3) Bought Iyanla's book, *Don't Give It Away*, because I'm not going to do that anymore, and I'm trying to build up my self-esteem like she talks about in the book

Gratitude

1) A free day

2) Finishing my counseling article

3) Having fun the previous two days

4) Doing things differently

8/4

Pampering

1) Took a nap in the afternoon instead of running around

2) Bought myself some new lip gloss

Gratitude

1) That I went to see the wonderful Carlos Santana yesterday

2) I had $ to buy travelers checks for my trip

8/5

Pampering

1) Went to Wilamena's picnic and had fun and insisted that my girlfriend drive, as we planned, when she tried to get me to drive

Gratitude

1) A free day tomorrow

2) A fun day today

8/6

Pampering

1) I had dinner by scented candlelight, listening to Diana Krall, eating Jersey tomatoes, fresh sweet scallops and that expensive pasta I bought to cook for Allen, which I will now never do

2) Did yoga finally

3) Bought myself two lipsticks and three hair clips

Gratitude

1) That I had a free day today

2) That I'm going to the Vigin Islands tomorrow

3) that God is good

8/7 - 11

Pampering

My trip to the Virgin Islands was one big pampering. I was grateful for so much.

1) Getting to know my old friend Joy again on our trip and enjoying her company

2) The beautiful beach and pool and hotel

3) Joy's father also being down in St. Thomas and showing us around

4) Seeing, and swimming in an underwater park; what a gorgeous, clear, unspoiled, hidden beach

5) Seeing Vince again after meeting him there on vacation 20 years ago and getting to know him again and the depth of the feelings he had for me

6) The fun, fun time I had on the booze cruise. I can't remember the last time I danced so much and so uninhibited, and got so drunk after two drinks. It must have been the combination of the sea and the liquor that did me in. But, whatever it was, I needed it and had a ball!

8/12

Pampering

I slept late and took a bath with candles.

Gratitude

My kids came home from camp safe and sound.

8/13

Pampering

1) I rented a video for me: *An Ideal Husband* (wish I could find one. Does he exist?)

2) Bought myself two new CDs and a boom box for my office

Gratitude

1) Was able to recover some free time when Tom took the kids to a baseball game

2) Allen called

3) The good feelings I have after spending that wonderful time in St. Thomas with Vince

8/14

Pampering

1) Bought myself some new incense ($1.91) and lit it while I did Ali McGraw's yoga tape, a different 45 minute treat

Gratitude

1) My kids being home safe

2) Putting out the fires at work

3) My health

4) My ability to pay my bills

8/15

Pampering

1) I called Vince. I just up and did it. Didn't wait for him to call. Wanted to get it over with and confirm that reconnecting with him after all this time

and this wonderful feeling that I have isn't a dream

Gratitude

1) Mom watching the kids so I could go to work

2) Getting a lot of work done at work

8/16

Pampering

1) Stopped working in the afternoon and took the kids to the pool; spent 4 hours there enjoying the sun and fun

2) Watched one of the movies I rented with the kids — *Anywhere But Here.* How appropriate.

3) Took a nap

Gratitude

1) A wonderful day at the pool

2) Watching a movie with my kids

3) Honoring myself first and letting work wait

8/17

Pampering

1) Bought a Duke Ellington Gold Live CD

2) Took the kids to McDs for lunch using the free cheeseburger coupons Angela got from the library's summer reading contest

Gratitude

1) The sister at McDs gave us free French fries when, after we looked in the bag, I told her that we had ordered them and that she forgot to give them to us

8/18

Pampering

1) Watched the movie, *The Matrix*, with the kids

2) Slept late

Gratitude

1) That I had time to watch the movie with the kids

2) The way my kids seem to love me

∂◆

8/19

Pampering

1) I went to my girlfriend's cookout instead of staying home and moping and doing the work I had to do, even though getting dressed for the cookout was an effort, but then I remembered "say something hat day" and my duty to myself to dress well and look as good as I can in spite of whatever else is going on, to not give in to my circumstances

Gratitude

1) That the kids got off safely on their trip to Mexico with Dad

2) That the kids were happy about their trip

3) That I had fun at the party bonding with the girls and meeting new girls

4) That I met a new guy at the cookout, Rick, who said he's going to take me to lunch — someone new to date? That would be nice. Actually, Rick isn't a new guy, and we've met before. He was in my same graduating class from college. I didn't really know him, but I did remember his face. Now he's separated and moved here last month from Atlanta to take a job as in-house counsel with a local corporation.

8/20

Pampering

1) I exercised when I could have stayed home and worked

2)   I went "down the house", the old family homestead — my late grand-mother's and grandfather's house, after church and visited my three aunts who still live there

Gratitude

1)   That I went to church and heard a good sermon

2)   I finished the book review I was writing for our local newspaper; this is a great accomplishment to be a published and paid book critic

8/21

Pampering

1)   I went to bed right after I came home from work because I didn't feel well

Gratitude

1)   Tom called from the town where he and the kids were vacationing. They were fine and having a good time and getting ready to go on to the next town.

2)   Rick called for a date; we're going out on Saturday

8/22

Pampering

1)   I left work, came home, got in bed and got the rest I needed

Gratitude

1)   Tom and the kids called. They're in Acapulco and on to Cancun and everything's fine

2)   The program I ran today at school for the new students was a great success, so, I hope that keeps my job secure for another year

3)   I met some very nice law students; a great group

8/23

Pampering

1) Again: came home and got in bed

Gratitude

1) That I have a job that lets me be flexible with my time

2) Takeout food

3) Mark, one of the computer guys at work, going the extra mile to fix my computer

8/24

Pampering

1) Again, I came home and got in bed

Gratitude

1) I had a nice lunch date with Rick

8/25

Pampering

1) I slowed down and talked on the phone to my good old friend George while I had lunch; what a fun conversation we had about my love life, or lack thereof, or maybe the one that is coming back

Gratitude

1) That I had dinner with Joy and we relived our trip to St. Thomas

2) Joy and I are renewing our friendship

3) That I at least found the negatives, if not the pictures, of my trip to the St. Thomas 20 years ago

4) That it's Friday

5) That all my responsibilities planning formal programs for the new students are over; I always get nervous that things are going to work out fine, but they always work out fine, so maybe next year I won't get so nervous

8/26

Pampering

1) I slept late

Gratitude

1) That I had a great time in the city at the picnic given one of my friends in city government, and that I reconnected with some people I used to work closely with years ago on the political battlefields but that I don't get to see very often now that I live in suburbia

8/27

Pampering

1) I went to see the movie *Saving Grace*, which was about a widow who finds herself without money and in great debt after her husband dies and how she gets herself out of financial trouble and unexpectedly finds herself a husband she is happy with, a story of great inspiration to me

Gratitude

1) For going to the oldies night at a nightclub downtown with another separated friend of mine and having a great time dancing up a storm — what fun!

2) For feeling better physically; I'm finally getting over the cold that has sent me to bed almost every night last week

8/28

Pampering

1) I took a bath before my date

Gratitude

1) For a nice date with Rick

8/29

Pampering

1) I took a nap before I went out

2) I had my hair weave taken out; enough of long hair that doesn't belong to me and high maintenance. I'm glad to have my hair back. To hell with anyone who doesn't like it because my hair is me, and I have to be accepted for me.

3) Went to a Diana Krall/Tony Bennett concert

Gratitude

1) That I went to the concert

2) The pictures that I made from my 20-year old St. Thomas trip negatives came out fine

3) That my hair grew and filled in some, enough for me to wear it out, free, natural, me

4) I like myself and am comfortable with myself just as I am

5) I am comfortable enough to wear my hair out

6) I checked on the enrollment for my course for next year and it is full; they like and trust me

8/30

Pampering

1)   ??? (I can't think of anything today)

Gratitude

1)   The kids' health teacher, who was in the counseling class that I started today, said my kids were great; that's nice to hear that my work has paid off

8/31

Pampering

1)   Bought some new hair care products, Mizani; which I wanted for a while and a new Billy Holiday CD — Greatest Hits

Gratitude

1)   Finished the law review article basically

2)   Went shopping with the kids, and they're happy about getting their back-to-school stuff

9/1

Pampering

1)   Bought two new CDs — Aretha (no last name required) and Omara Portuna

2)   Hung out at the bookstore with Angela

Gratitude

1)   Sent the article off

2)   It's Friday

3)   Angela felt close enough to me to want to spend the night in my room

9/2

Pampering

1) Bought a pleather trench coat, very modern and hip

2) Bought some new hair care stuff

Gratitude

1) My kids are as great as they are

9/6

Pampering

1) Bought Buena Vista Social Club CD and Oprah's new book club book

Gratitude

1) Had lunch with Rick; was very nice

2) That I got up the nerve to call Rick that night since he's been calling me so often, and I so enjoyed having lunch with him today

3) My kids

9/7

Pampering

1) Took myself to dinner at an Indian restaurant between dropping/picking up kids at various things

Gratitude

1) That I called Donald; I didn't think that he had called me the day he was leaving the National Convention, but he had called me; I just never got the message. He said that he wants to see me again.

2) My kids

9/8

Pampering

1)   Took a nap when I came home

Gratitude

1)   It's Friday!

CHAPTER 17
THIS IS THE WAY, WALK YE IN IT

9/9

I JUST CAME ACROSS a great scripture — Isaiah 30:20, 21.

20: *And though the Lord give you the bread of adversity, and the water of afflic-tion, yet shall not thy teachers be removed in a corner any more, but thine eyes shall see thy teachers.*

21: *And thine ears shall hear a word behind thee, saying, this is the way, walk ye in it, when ye turn to the right hand, and when ye turn to the left.*

Also *Romans 8:28, 31, 32, 35 - 39*; actually all of Ch. 8 is excellent. About how Jesus overcame the law, which is flesh bound to sin and to death, to give us grace and everlasting life and all good things. So Christians should be happy with what God did for us through Jesus, because the law wasn't working, and He wanted to give us all good things, so He sent his son, and He gave us the good things through his death and resurrection; so we as Christians should be happy, faith-filled and not complaining because Jesus truly paid it all.

How much better I feel! I never really understood this before in my soul and in my very being. Now that I do, I'm wondering: what am I complaining about? I am saved and God wants all good things for me and sacrificed his son to give them to me.

As He says in *Romans 8:32* —

He that spared not his own Son, but delivered Him up for us all, how shall He not with him also freely give us all things.

31: *What shall we then say to these things? If God be for us, who can be against us?*

37: Nay, in all these things we are more than conquerors, through Him that loved us.

38-39: For I am persuaded, that neither death, nor life, nor angels, nor principalities, nor powers, nor things present, nor things to come, nor height, nor depth, nor any other creature, shall be able to separate us from the love of God, which is in Christ Jesus our Lord.

Meaning: whatever comes or is thrown our way cannot separate us from God and all of his goodness and the good things he has planned for us.

The lesson I got from this is to keep my eye and mind and heart on God, and I'll feel and be alright.

9/10

Happy Birthday! I've found the I Ching's words and sentiment to be quite soothing. These are my I Chings for today:

    _____ _____ 811

    _____ _____ 8

    _____ _____64th line

    _____7

    _____7

Interpreted, this means: Peace. "The mean decline; the great and good approach — good fortune and success!" Great. Maybe this year will be a good one.

    _____ _____

    _____ _____34

    _____

    _____

_____

_____

This means : "The Power of the Great. Persistence in a righteous course brings reward." More good news. I'm on a roll. (Reminder: check back in a year whether this prediction was true.)

9/24

I feel out of sorts. I don't know what my sorts are, but I feel out of them.

9/26

The realization that I must move has hit me. The weight of what I have to do depressed me. But today — guess what! — I got pre-approved for a mortgage of up to $400,000 if I put 25% down. Little old me!

And I was worried about my credit rating. Well, I got an A credit rating. 6.4 was the minimum for an A rating; mine is 7.42. I did it! I did better than I thought! I can handle this! I can make it work.

è**

9/28

Dear Vince,

I'm writing this letter since you live so far away from me and since you're married, I can't just pick up the phone and call you when I want to. I want to share so much with you but can't. The words are stuck in my throat. Like taffy/like cotton candy that won't dissolve. They expand to fill the space available and the time that I am away from you. I'll wait until I can see you again. By that time, I'll have so much to tell you, all I will be able to say is "I love you."

The realization that I must move hit me. And that I must do it alone. I wish I could do it with you. I wish you were here to help me. I wish you were here to live with me. I wish.

9/29

Dear Vince,

Why can't you live here! In my continuing attempts to get on with my life, I have a date tonight with Rick. But now my friend tells me that this guy has been lying to me about some very fundamental stuff, like whether he is truly separated from his wife, although it appeared to me that he was since he lived here in Massachusetts and she lives in Atlanta. I don't know who to believe. But I feel stupid and I feel the pain and ache of betrayal moving up my spine and lodging itself in my neck as big time tension.

If you were here, I wouldn't have to think about this. I could just be with you. I wouldn't believe anyone but you. I wouldn't have to. He doesn't make me feel the way that you do. I know this is a rescue fantasy, but so what. With Rick, there's not an instant comfort level like there was with me and you. We're not instantly physically compatible. The one time we had sex was such a dud; the fastest ever; over and done in about two seconds — literally. Just when I thought that I could relax enough to trust him, to let myself be comfortable with him physically, this disturbing news of betrayal pops up. I'm wondering whether I should go ahead and relax anyway, or should I pull back. I'm tired of pulling back, though, because that means death to my physical desires until someone else appears. I did it for two years, and I guess I could do it again, but I don't want to.

You awakened something in me and let me see how beautiful everything could be. I hope to trust someone the way I trust you. I hope that someone can make me feel the way that you do.

You are all these things. God knows I wish that I could have a life with you that was more than an occasional meeting. I wish I had a day-to-day spectacular kind of love and sex on an everyday basis. That would thrill me to no end. I don't want substitutes. But then I think that I'm being delusional with you — a married man thousands of miles away who hasn't even called me (or written I suppose) since the two weeks he came up to visit me and we made fabulous love and declared our love for each other. One day, everything will come together for me.

In the meantime, I obsess about things. I shy away from being hurt. I'm afraid of being vulnerable at the same time I want to take risks. I want to give all that love that is welled up inside of me. It seems that I have a hard time doing that.

10/2

Dear Vince,

I miss you so much! My trust was misplaced. It turns out that Rick really had asked to sleep with my friend when he told me and my cousin that he had no interest whatsoever in her. Here I am trying to trust someone (because you are not around) and he turns out to be a liar. Don't I feel stupid!

But, as my therapist says, be open, first, and take a risk, but then when you see or experience something that is not right, get out. Know what you want. Know what your standards are. Don't lower them.

As Maya Angelou said, "When someone shows you who they are, believe them the first time." The lesson is — don't wait around for a second time when you are deeper in it and have so much invested that it's harder to get out. Why can't I do that easily?

Fear! Fear that I have no one else here. That no one else will come along. That something is better than nothing.

But, anyway, it all feels like hell. I get a headache just thinking about it.

10/4

I am becoming a pod person. My pod is growing again, like a protective covering. I was out in the world and got hurt. I need protection from being overwhelmed by life. The pod has to be strong enough to protect me from men who try to hurt me. With the pod, I can interact with them, but they can't touch me, can't reach me, my soul or my body. And all the people who try to hurt me and overwhelm me can't get to the real me.

My fantasy is to have my pod shoot darts or poisonous juices at those who try to hurt me. Zap! They shrink back. They leave me alone. They try another target.

I stay inside my pod, I grow inside my pod, I get strong inside my pod until it's time to come out. Lord knows when that will be, because I don't.

10/5

The latest self-help tome that I'm reading is *The Comfort Queen* by Jennifer Louden.

That's all about answering certain questions. Here goes:

1) What is the one thing I need more of in my life right now?
Answer: Love. No question about it.

2) What one modest step am I willing to take to get more love into my life?
Answer: To be more open to it, to be me, unafraid of me, to be contented with me, to not worry about it.

3) What do I need less of in my life?
Answer: Clutter.

4) What one modest step am I willing to take to decrease one of these things in my life?
Answer: Clean my house and office.

10/11 — Question 2 — 1:21 a.m.

1) What are my most common obstacles to relaxation and self-nurturing now?

Answer: Lack of time, misplaced priorities, pressing needs (house decisions), guilt, meeting my children's needs, housework, being scatterbrained and disorganized, the drive to achieve, true desire.

10/12

Gratitude

1) My foot is not broken, like Darlene, who was just standing on the boardwalk down the Shore and some kid on a skateboard ran into her foot and shattered it and now she is out of work for a few months while she goes through foot rehab.

2) I am healthy

3) The visit from the law student I mentor

4) I saw Angela's field hockey game

5) My son's smile

10/16

Thoughts.

HERE I AM, 45 YEARS OLD, still worried about trying to figure out men. Yet, at the same time, I am concerned about my daughter, about to turn 13, about to be really interested in boys, starting to try to figure out young men and hoping she doesn't get hurt. I think it's my duty as a Mom to impart some wisdom to her, to tell her something about men, to try to help her understand men, but I realize that I can't. How can I help her when I consider myself a failure? How can I help her, what can I tell her, when I failed at marriage and when I'm failing at dating because a wonderful man hasn't shown up yet?

Every guy I date, something comes up. Dating is like walking through a field with hidden land mines. Everything looks safe and you're walking right along thinking it's all A OK when you step out, and boom! A land mine that was buried beneath the surface explodes and hurts you, maims you, forcing you to go somewhere for treatment (mental), somewhere to heal. I feel like I should do like Princess Diana did, walk around with a mask on, protecting myself, knowing the land mines are there, but just not where.

I feel like I've let my daughter down. She now has to make sense of adolescence and men alone. A mother's job is to help her kids. How can I help mine, and why should they listen to me? This, potentially, is one of the worst consequences of divorce. As much as I try to be a good mother, I can't on this one. I'm sending them out there adrift. They don't have an image of a loving relationship to look to. Mom and Dad divorced. Uncle and Aunt divorced.

Grand mom and Grand pop do nothing but fight.

Up to now, they have adjusted. This has been what they've known and seen, and I thought that they were young enough so that it does not/did not make a difference. Maybe I've been in denial about that. But now I know that it does make a difference, will make a difference.

I feel like I need to stop trying to save the world with the community groups that I am involved in and solely focus on saving my children. They will need me/do need me. Not much else really matters in the long run and maybe in the short run. Can I give up a lot of other things in my life and just focus on them? Should I? Will it make a difference? Does what I do with other groups make a difference? Do I dare drop out of sight again, like I did when they were small after I swam with the political sharks and they ate me alive? Can I? Should I? Who would care if I didn't do something, didn't so-called "get a life"?

I tend to think that I worry about the wrong things. All I can do is take care of myself and my kids, I think. Everything else seems to be too hard. So, here's my life plan — only do those things that I — singularly — enjoy and that are good for me. Those things include — going to the movies, doing yoga, occasionally seeing a play, reading and discussing books, hanging out at home/relaxing at home with people I enjoy, not trying to impress anyone.

10/16

Men are like those ink fish that look good and appealing on the outside, so you get closer, closer and closer, then you touch them and are shocked when they shoot ink all over you.

ↄ

Another bad two entry-day.

Maybe I'll turn into one of those women who don't date. Who have pushed men out of their lives because it's too hard otherwise. I've always felt sorry for those women, wondered how they could do it, and never thought that would be me one day. I thought I was better than that. But it turns out that I may not be. I just wonder why I haven't been able to have the relationship happiness in my life that I seek. Why I have to be taught certain lessons. It does feel like a punishment. Every time I think I'm going in the right direction, I'm not. I'm not good at the game and need to honest about that. So, I guess I'll stop playing the game. Withdrawal. Be cold. Act like it doesn't matter. Fake it until I can make it. Just go on. Don't be bothered. Don't put myself out there. Keep fear away from me. Protect myself. I guess I have to because no one else will.

It's kind of like — who do I think I am? Why do I think I'm so special that I have a right to be happy?

Or maybe it's just about trusting myself and sticking to my convictions. Let's just take the men, run them down, list why I know the relationship was wrong, when I knew it, why I went ahead with it anyway, why I was surprised when I got hurt:

— *Allen*: Vast age difference. Slept with him on first date. Did not seem so accommodating to my schedule. Saw mean and cruel streak. Did not give me feedback on my book, my prize, one of the most important things I've done with my life. Wasn't there when I needed him (didn't come to my party or RSVP). Rejected me.

— *Vince*: Married. Lives thousands of miles away. Didn't write or call on his own initiative. Indicates lack of concern for me and my feelings because I cannot write/call him at home.

— *Rick*: First thing on mind — sex. Still married. Newly separated. Hundreds of ties to home. Liar. Insensitive and unsatisfying lover. Let me down. Left me hanging. Disrespected me. Did not take my feelings into consideration.

— Donald: Said he'd call but didn't (several times). Philosophically very different. Afraid of commitment and sex — I think.

I have been hurt and disappointed by all of them. Why don't I just tell them all that I can't see them anymore? Why don't I just end it with them all? What am I afraid of?

10/19

More Comfort Queen questions

Q: In the next month, what two or three places do I feel the most stress? What has me in knots? What makes me lose my temper?

— When I have to sit through a boring, bureaucratic Jack & Jill meeting; when I have to look at/live in clutter in my house; when I have to go on recruiting trips for my job and leave my kids and my home.

Q: How can I nurture myself in the days ahead?

— Cut one thing from my daily calendar; take baths; go to the movies

— Clean my house

— Listen to music

— Read good books for pure enjoyment

— Drink coconut rum and coke and relive my vacation

— Do yoga everyday; give myself that gift

— Be better organized

Q: How have I been talking to myself?

— Like sometimes I've given up hope

— At other times, like I know precisely what to do, but I'm not doing it

— Honestly and in a straightforward manner

10/24

I feel such a need to detach from what I've been doing so that I can find the true, authentic me. I need to slow down, look around, explore, and stop being so damned responsible for everyone and everything and being the one who keeps it all together (whatever it is, which often seems to be everything under the sun). I need a vacation, a change of scenery — but where?

10/25

No one calls me, and I feel like I'm being transported to another world. I am not of this one. The one I knew is changing. It's not supposed to be like this. People are supposed to care. But they don't. So I'm leaving them. Or they've left me, and I just now realize it. The silence is deafening, yet telling. I'm not popular, but I like it. Because I'm tired. Tired of calls that interrupt my silence, that pick at me, that lead me to expectations that disappear, dissipate and frustrate. So I accept the silence. I try to embrace it because I believe that it's leading me to something else.

My illusions about others are leaving me. When I find myself thinking that they do care, I embrace the silence in a strangely comforting way and know that they don't. Maybe I'm waking up, accepting reality, seeing these people for what they really are. Then maybe I'll move them out of my life, stop devoting so much psychic energy to people who aren't really there, like a black hole, and move on, make space for people who will be there.

Thoughts on my writing:

I have to be a little crazy to write. A little off. Very much in touch with my unconventional side, which I should just let come out, maybe through these journals. Maybe when I feel like saying something, but don't, but can't, if I write it down, I won't get any more crazy, won't repress, won't implode. Maybe that's been my problem. Blocked craziness pushing to get out. Acting up inside until released. And if not released, it keeps pushing and trying to come out, but if it doesn't come out as emotion, it comes out as back pain, acne, neck strain and worse.

Thoughts on my friends, or lack thereof:

I have to stop thinking of my friends because they're not there. Don't exist. Figments. I stand in search of reality. I don't want to be bound by the past, putting energy into relationships that have served their purpose. I should be happy that they have. There are lots of people in the big world out there. I need to make room for them.

⌒

Second entry. (We're descending into the maelstrom here.)

Waiting for phone calls. How awful.

There's no clearer evidence than the lack of a phone call that someone doesn't care. Doesn't care to share his life with you or doesn't care about how your life is going. There are no excuses and no way around it. Especially if they have your home phone number, your work phone number, and your cell phone number. Three ways to reach you. If someone doesn't call me to find out how my day went, he doesn't really care about me. Period. End of story. No need to make excuses or sugarcoat it. Men go after what they want, when they want it. The rest is bullshit. I have to accept and understand that.

But why do I get such an empty feeling in the pit of my stomach when someone who I think is flawed, who I've even contemplated not dating, does-n't call. Because of expectancies. I still expect them to be interested in me. I don't expect them to see the flaws in me and think that they don't want to date me or talk to me. Of course they should want to do both. Maybe what creates the pit is the realization that I'm not all that, and no matter how hard I try re: behavior, looks, sex, I am not/cannot be all that to some of the peo-ple I'd like to be all that to (bad grammar, but you know what I mean). So, the best I can do is be myself and stop worrying.

I pray everyday to stop worrying, to stop needing someone and his acceptance, to not desire sex, to be self-contained until I am blessed with the right man. Maybe that is really what I ought to focus on. I keep coming back to that. That I should just move the men out of my life because it hurts too much to not have the right one in there. I think I need to just focus on being me, putting me first, doing what appeals to me, saying what I want to say no matter how it comes across to anyone else. Good move. Good start.

I also need a change of scenery. A vacation. It's not going to just plop down on me. I have to take it.

☾

Third entry today (The descent is over; we are certifiably in the maelstrom.)

Again, waiting for a call. This is getting really redundant. A call as evidence that one of these mother fuckers really cares. I build my life around waiting for their calls. And now I wait for their emails. Another form of torture. I don't know why I don't just let go and move on. There are other men out there! Clear out a space for them. Stop worrying about them coming in. Stop obsessing about it. If they want to come in, they will. God will drop them down from the sky, right and ready.

Another thing I'm doing, or have done, is to obsess (or what to me is obsession) re: Rick.

I wait for a call or email from him, someone I essentially told not to call or email me. That was then. This is now. I may be schizophrenic, but he doesn't have to believe it. I was in control then. I'm not in control now. He said he'd call me, and he didn't. I told him to stay away, let him step away, but now I wish he was back closer. I feel like I had to let him get away for him to come back the right way — whatever that is. I do miss him. Do realize how good he was to me. The fact that he wanted to be with me was/is good enough. And that he treated me like a queen, of sorts, paying for whatever we did, which was whatever I wanted, and that he pursued me. I had/have a massive fear of being hurt. Am I taking that out on him, or is my reaction natural and justified re: how he's treated me, what he hid from me?

10/26

This vision just came to me.

The men in my life are observers, not participants, in this vision. It is like I am in a little room with several windows and one door. I am sitting in the middle of the room in a chair and there's an empty chair beside me. The men's activity disturbs me. All day long they come in and out of the door. They see me, I look interesting, so they walk in the room, some stay close to the door, look at me, watch what I'm doing, hoping to see me do what (entertain them?), (make a mistake?), I do not know. They've had enough. They don't like what they see, and they leave.

Others come in and walk around, looking at me the whole time, come closer, try to get a closer look, disturbing me with their activity, and then they leave, walk back out, the sounds of their hollow footsteps reverberate off the walls and ring in my ears long after they've left. And then there are the timid ones. I see them looking in the window, faces pressed against the glass, interested in my world, inspecting me, making their presence known on my radar screen, making sure I see them there, wondering why they don't come in, disturbing me, becoming bored, disinterested, or rejecting what they see after pressing their faces against the glass, dirtying it, disturbing me, leaving their imprint for me to clean up. When what I really want is for someone to come in, sit down beside me, stay with me and experience life as I see it, beside me, engaging in the physiological act of seeing the world as I do, sharing with me the experience of being in that room, in the world, in my life. Finding that chair easy and comfortable and not leaving. Maybe getting up to lock the door and close the curtains so no one else can disturb us.

Second entry. This is either despair or awareness;
either way, I'm really feeling a lot of stuff.

4:23 a.m.

Or, I envision the men as little toys, little dolls, miniature people who, when I am finished playing with them, or when I realize the depths of their insincerity or nonattachment to me, I pick up and place on a shelf with the other miniature people I don't want to be bothered with right now. I envision them as just sitting there, not speaking, not moving, giving the appearance that they're looking at me, but not really; as dead to me as a toy is.

When I feel that I miss them or when I feel bad that they are not in my life, were not "the one" or at least "the one for now", I visualize them on the shelf, their useful life, at least to me, finished.

Or, they're like products that have passed their expiration dates. Only good until the third date, then they are of no more use to you, they go bad, they spoil, they've worn out. So, don't use them past that date because there's no useful life there, their rottenness will hurt you. Get another one.

Sometimes I think I should throw those toys into a box. Put them away for a while where, like a two-year-old with little memory, I can forget about them until Mommy drags out that box because I'm bored with my other toys, and I can look at those old toys with fresh eyes — I realize that I missed them, that I have affection for them, that I'm excited to see them again, that I want to play with them again.

Or maybe I should just give the toys away to another woman and let her play with them.

Or act like a mature woman and declutter. Give the box away, unblock the feelings. Holding on to old, worn out stuff blocks the blessings in Feng Shui theory. Eventually, I'll get tired of looking at the old box, catching dust and taking up space, and give it away and hope for something new/plan for something new/make space for something new.

☙

My mantra, thanks to one of Iyanla Vanzant's wonderful books, which one, I can't remember, because I've read every one and gotten so much out of all of them:

Today I surrender, I release, I detach from every person, every circumstance, every condition, and every situation that no longer serves a divine purpose in my life!

10/27

The Questions (6) (more Comfort Queen stuff)

1) Yes — I am calming others fears when I need to be calming my own

2) Being kind and gentle and forgiving with myself; pampering myself

3) Yes. It would feel great to get out of my own way.

4) Be confident. Pamper myself. Treat myself like someone cares about me, like someone is watching me. I would hold my head up. I would walk with pride and confidence in myself and all that I do.

10/28 5:18 a.m.

I miss Rick. I don't like dealing with the emptiness. It haunts me throughout the day. I think of him. I want to call and reach out but then I think I'll be pulled deeper into the abyss, having already offered myself on my own terms and being told, "no thanks; not that way." Reaching out is compromise. Is settling. Is giving in. Or is it? Or is it working with what is, knowing that it's not now all that I want, hoping that one day it will be. Is it better to be hurt now or hurt later? Better to get over the hurt now or get over it later. Seems like the best thing to do is to leave it alone and ride it out. He said he'd be dating others but also would want to be with me. So, is he compromising, but not letting grass grow under his feet? Is it easy for him to move on from me to someone else?

.: Undated notes :.

Indecision pounds inside my head. Punching at the walls of my brain, trying to get me to decide. Be open and call him. Tell him that I miss him. No, don't. Don't let him know how I feel. Wait it out. It's a game. Let him call me. He said he would. Don't let him know that I miss him, that I appreciated all the attention that he gave me, that I appreciated the honesty; those times he was honest, that sometimes I could see him bearing every layer of his soul, trusting me because he wanted me. Don't let him know that maybe I'm changing my view, not being so rigid and dogmatic about him, not filing him into every one of the categories that I usually file men into before I give them some play. The call maybe indicates that I am ready to accept him for who he is, be grateful for who he is, go by how he treats me, because the bottom line is… he is the one who was there, who is there.

10/29

I bought *Women Who Run with the Wolves* because Alice Walker said that was one of her most favorite books. I want to be like/write like Alice Walker.

CHAPTER 20
NO NEED TO STAY IN THE MUCK AND MIRE

10/30

MY SON'S SPIRIT SOARS like those feather light white things that the petals of a dandelion turn into. He doesn't stay down. A visiting three-year-old that Angela was babysitting for messed up his favorite PlayStation game. He pouted for a while. Was sad. But then he got on the computer. The next day he tried to fix the game, to test it, and it still didn't work. So he moved on. The funk was gone.

At breakfast 10 minutes later, he was sunny, happy, his usual upbeat self. And he stayed that way all day. No need to stay in the muck and mire obsessing about something he can't change. There was a big, interesting, fun world out there and he wanted to have fun in it. So he moved on to baseball, roller blades, his skateboard, and he had a ball. Why can't I be like him? Like that? He has my genes. He comes from me. His is me — extended. Thirty four years difference and a whole ton of experiences has made me someone who obsesses, who gets stuck, who finds it difficult to move on and have fun. I want to be like him. And a little child shall lead them.

11/1

Why did I get so upset today when the parking bitches at that school in Florida where I was recruiting made me park my car at the satellite parking lot, take their tired, broken down van up to the student center a half-mile away, go inside the student center to get the parking pass, and then wait for a van to take me back down to the parking lot. Then I got ugly with them when the van didn't come after about 20 minutes, so I made them get another student to give me a ride, and then the parking bitches got an attitude because I got an attitude about their ridiculous parking rules. So, I immediately formed an opinion that the whole situation was bullshit and, of course the parking bitches acted this way because, after all, the town where the college is located is nothing but a backwater.

The reality:

That I want to be liked is at the bottom of it. I expect things to go a certain way. I know they could go more smoothly. I don't like the way they are going/operating. I know I could do better. Don't they realize who I am? How valuable my time is? What a sacrifice I even made to get here? How backwater they are? But what really gets me is that I bought into the system. I took the stupid pass even though I disagreed with it and thought I had handled the situation my way. That's it. I had determined that the system was so ridiculous that I wasn't even going to get involved in it, but then I didn't stick with my thinking and got mad at myself for buying into someone else's view of things. So, it wasn't their fault. They were just doing their jobs.

But now they have a certain opinion of me. Now I'm "that bitch who railed about the parking." But why do I care? I'm sure I'm not the only one who railed about the parking, although I was probably the first one since I got there before most of the other recruiters.

I'll probably never see those people again, although I will see them until 4 o'clock today when this recruiting fair is over. I'd like to forget this unfortunate incident. Give it up to God and ask for healing.

Should I ask for their forgiveness for my attitude? I don't think so. I am who I am, and I'm not going to apologize for it. Maybe I will just accept my wild/shadow nature (having just read and been highly influenced by *Women Who Run With the Wolves*).

Maybe what bothers me is that my wild, shadow nature has reared its head — ugly or not. So, I shouldn't be afraid to look any of them in the eye, to smile later — if I feel like it, if our paths cross. I'm not perfect. I don't act perfectly. I probably should just learn to forgive and forget. Like my son. When it's done, it's done. He moves on to the next thing. Forgetting what lies behind. Forgiving himself. Forgiving others.

11/6

First, honoring my creative instincts, I am writing. Came in to work today — varied my format. Instead of 20 minutes of mediation, which relaxes me and calms me, I launched into my work, got some things done. I will meditate soon, because I feel myself getting nervous.

I am so scattered, so all over, so responding to this unseen force that is looking over me, judging my work, making me attend to certain things when that unseen judge is really me. I feel that I am in a "learning/passive mode", not an "active/productive in a big sense mode"--this mode stuff coming from another self-help book.

Anyway, onward and upward and on to my novel — but will I work on the one that's been kicking around for the past few years, or the one that feels right?

11/7

The comfort/assurance that I thought I had was a lie in so many ways. The illusion that if I was a "good wife", whatever that means, my marriage would last. The illusion that my husband knew what he was doing and was competent to take care of me, the children, this home.

I put my trust in Tom. Believed that he knew how to take care of a house because he already had one when we met, and, besides, he was a man, and men knew these things, didn't they? I thought they did, but I guess I didn't know for sure, only having my father around until I was four years old and not remembering anything he did, not having a man around, my mother being the one who was doing everything. But I digress.

Another instance of having the rug, my illusion of security snatched out from under me. When Tom left, he left all responsibility for this big house on me. He didn't lift a finger to do anything around here. He didn't care about me. He didn't care about the house. I tried to keep things going as best as I could. I paid bills when they came in; I fixed things when they broke, but I deferred maintenance big time. If it wasn't broken, I didn't take care of it. I had to conserve whatever $ I had, not knowing what I was going to end up with.

But I read. I read about home maintenance because it was all on me. I had an idea of what I should do. Cleaning furnace filters was one thing. He never showed me how to do it, or told me that it had to be done. He just wanted to get me out of this house as fast as he could. Forget the fact that his kids lived here, his asthmatic child who needed clean air. So, when the dust settled from the settlement, and I realized that I could not defer maintenance any more, because there were things that had to be done to get the house ready for sale, like fix the leak in the dining room ceiling that dripped water on the antique oak dining room table that he was going to take with him. So, I had to call the plumber. The painter couldn't paint the dining room ceiling until the leak was fixed. And we couldn't put the house on the market until that ceiling and many other interior walls were painted.

So I asked the plumber to look at the heater, to check the filters, to determine why the house was so cold in spots. So he looked. And what he found astounded me and hit me in the stomach. The heater/air cleaner filter was clogged with so much dirt and dust it was probably working at 2% efficiency. You were supposed to be able to see through the wire mesh filters. We could not. So he washed them out and asked, "These haven't been cleaned in a while? Since you lived here"? And I said, "My husband was so bad about things like that. I know I haven't cleaned them, and it's been two to three years." Out of curiosity and embarrassment, I asked, how often should they be cleaned, and he said every two to three months. And he said, since they were cleaned, I'd see a big difference as far as air flow and efficiency. Maybe my bedroom wouldn't be so cold after all.

Now, one of the good things about this house was the air cleaner and the efficient heating system. Unbeknownst to me, the air cleaner hadn't been working for years. No wonder Angela's asthma was getting worse. Maybe having a working air cleaner will help her get better.

So the plumber kept checking things out. Then he found out that the valve in the humidifier was not drawing in water like it should for the humidifier to work. Again, dirty air, dry nasal passages, more colds and illnesses. I felt stupid but I thought that Tom had taken care of these things. I also felt let down again. More evidence that Tom didn't know what he was doing, that he was in over his head when he bought this big ass house.

And what about me? I trusted him and let him take care of the house and the finances while I took care of the babies. But if I had paid any attention to the house and finances, things wouldn't be the way they are. But I didn't. I gave it up to sex-role stereotyping. I think I should have known better, but I didn't, so I did the best I could have. Now I know better, so now I'll do better.

More evidence that women can't give up their lives to a man. Or that I just picked the wrong man. In deciding whether to marry him, I looked at other things besides his ability to take care of a home (or lack thereof). Maybe men should learn more about taking care of the kids.

I had always felt a bit insecure about Tom's ability to handle things around the house, his lack of attention to detail. But I always thought that he would handle things eventually so I didn't have to be too concerned. Boy, was I wrong.

Then this raises all types of feelings like, here we go, Black women can't depend on Black men to take care of them, at least can't depend on them to do it the right way. That it's white women who get that. Or maybe they're not being taken care of in the same way that I wasn't being taken care of when it looked like I was, and the illusion still exists and is fostered by outward appearances. Land mines again. You don't know it's there until you step on it. Embedded in the dirt, hidden under the grass. The land mine can stay there for a while, but eventually the material that is covering it up wears away and surprises you. That's the title of my "going on after divorce" book — *Land Mines.*

11/13

The challenge is to stay grounded/centered. To be secure in myself. To be happy that I am in my right mind, have a good portion of health and strength, as the old folks say, relatively financially secure and blessed, blessed with two wonderful children and warm and secure shelter.

Rather than grasping, empty and disappointed. Waiting for a phone call from a man. Waiting for a man to care enough about me to call. Looking for that red light on my phone. That name in the "From" column on my email. That masculine voice that answers back when I pickup the phone and say hello, rather than being disappointed when I hear the high, soft tones of a woman.

It's Monday morning. I haven't heard from Rick since Thursday. I imagine he went home this weekend, so that's why he didn't call (it's not his way to call when he is home with his children and wife). And I excuse his not calling on Friday by saying that he had a busy day, so busy he didn't have time to stop and call before he caught his plane that night, although I know this isn't true because he is a man who always carries his cell phone with him, who could always find a few minutes to make any phone call that he choose to make, which is any man's way. People, especially men, find time to do what they want to do.

My rationalizations make me sick. So does the silence. I want someone to care, and, in my delusional state, hoping against hope, I think that I can do something about that. Have some influence on a man. Make him want to call me. I see an ad for leather pants in the paper. Think about buying them to make myself more attractive, more sexy, more hip. Then I stop. I already am sexy, attractive and hip. I already look good, and what does it matter? Rick can screw me and then walk away, not call, all cool, calm and collected. How far must I go to try to draw him in? The futility of it. Buying the leather pants would get me more in debt, not get him to be more into me. There's nothing I can do, and I'm tired of even having my energy drained in the direction of wanting to do anything.

If I didn't want sex and a lover who wasn't screwing around, I would be fine. I could do what I so often feel the need to do, which is to leave alone all men who aren't serious about me, which turns out to be everyone that I am involved with.

I wish I could tell them with no fear and the conviction I often feel in my head because of the pain I often feel in my heart -- don't call me; I think it's best that we don't see each other. But I'm afraid that if I say that, they won't call back, won't come back. That they'll go away and there will be no one to replace them, and that I'll go through my round of loneliness again.

But I also realize that I get a bit crazy about all of this. That getting crazy about it is a sign that I'm not ready. I said that now, I'm going to not be bound my by fears, to jump in, go with the good feelings, work out the confusion and hurt with the one who is doing the hurting, rather than working it out alone.

I feel like I just have to stop. To stop wanting a good man. To stop worrying about a good man. To trust the state that I am in, the process of all this, where I am on this journey. To realize that where I am is where I should be, and that it's all good.

It's really all about surrender. I need to surrender, go with the flow and trust the flow. Not worry about what isn't; stay in the flow of what is, painful or not, to find the pleasure there. To not worry. To realize that all will turn out. But it's not "all" that I'm worried about or concerned about — it's love. I need to believe that my true love will find me, that I don't need to twist and torture anyone to get true love, and to realize that it may come to me differently than it's come to others.

❧

CHAPTER 21
ME? CHEMICALLY IMBALANCED?

11/17

DEPRESSION. MY THERAPIST — who I have been seeing for 2–3 years — tells me I'm depressed, and that depresses me. I don't know why. I know I'm depressed. That's why I go to counseling. Maybe she says it now because she doesn't see me making progress or questions the progress/or lack thereof/that I'm making. I thought I was doing good. Had made some worthwhile and reasoned changes — changed churches, stopped fearing Rick, started having sex, actively building the life I want to have instead of hiding from the one I have.

But depressed for real? Me? Chemically imbalanced? It ruins my image of myself as superwoman, someone who has it all together when I guess I don't. Depressed? That label is not a good reward for all of the work that I do. The hard work I've done to be better, to take it day-by-day, to put one foot in front of the other.

Maybe I'm a functioning depressive, like a functional alcoholic. I don't just stay in bed with the covers over me — although some days I'd like to. I get up and do what has to be done. Maybe it's gotten to the point where I can't play the game like I used to play it — I know that. I feel like throwing up my hands in defeat. I've tried. I am trying. I'll keep trying, but why? To what avail? When it seems like I'm still not doing the "right" thing, no matter what the "right" thing is. I feel jealous. Others look happy. Why can't I have it together like them, when I know appearances are deceiving and not everyone who looks like she has it together does in fact have it together.

I feel a need to be kind to myself. To get away. But isn't that a symptom of depression? Why can't I just be happy?

11/18

Depression. I wonder if my depression is the result of being in a bad marriage for 14 years, or is it me? Is it because I was married to such a difficult man for so long, a man who did not feed my soul the way it needed to be fed, who disrespected and belittled me, or is it the result of all kinds of chemical shit playing around in my head? Or is it that I'm not trying hard enough?

I'm convinced that it's not that I'm not trying enough; I try very hard. No matter how hard I try it seems that I can't lift myself out. Even with earnest prayers.

I know part of it is that I'm feeling sorry for myself. Sorry that my vision of my life did not work. Sorry that I married a man who was not there for me in so many ways. I am awakening in so many ways, sex just being one of them. I enjoy it so much more and am so much more free. I wonder if it's because the men are better lovers, or am I, or is it because I had so many years of horrible sex that I can appreciate when something is good?

Anyway, back to the depression. All of those years with a man who treated you badly, who drove you crazy, who was never satisfied, who was angry so much — that's enough to drive anyone crazy. Then in the separation/divorce, he let loose so much venom and hatred, not giving me any money for the kids for three months (something from which I'm still trying to recover financially), fighting me on everything, not respecting the contribution I made to raising the children, allowing him to go and work all hours of the day. I wish I could act in the "me first" attitude that he does. I know I need to do some more of that, but how much more exactly, I don't know.

I do know, that as Fannie Lou Hamer said, I'm sick and tired of being sick and tired. I hate being sad. Feeling that I have a headache that will not end. I have tried in every way I could think of to hold it together, to do better. If it doesn't have to be this hard, why am I making it so? If Prozac combined with what I'm already doing will lift this cloud, as my therapist thinks, then why do I fight it? I think I'd be crazy not to do it. So I guess I'll go see the shrink.

11/20

Question 12 (from The Comfort Queen*). How would I describe my life right now?*

I am in a job that I feel that I have outgrown. I am in a job that demands that I give more to other people than I want to. I am divorced, a single mom, trying to figure out how to make it. Unsure. Confused. Yet proud of myself for how far I've come and how well I've kept it together. I am often worn out and overwhelmed as my mind races forward. I'd like to make my house one that is comfortable for me. Every room.

11/21

What to write about today? Why am I not finishing my second novel? It remains unwritten, and I remain bored with it. What to do now? Write about something else? Why don't I just go with the flow and write what I feel like writing. When I have time, I'll put it all together.

11/24 — 2:59 a.m.

Where am I? What am I?

I am afraid of marriage because when a woman marries, she becomes domesticated. Just like an animal. She is tamed. Her wildness is taken out of her, beaten out of her, forced out of her. Just like a pet, so she can go on to fulfill her master's dreams. To exist for her master's pleasures. To make him feel comfortable. To make him feel better about himself because he is taking care of her. She allows him to show to the world that he is responsible (taking care of her/arranging for her care), and kind (providing her with food and a home). He gets the companionship he seeks, petting her, stroking her, to make him feel good, to feel the softness of her hair/fur, the way she snuggles up against him and is eternally grateful and loyal for what he has done for her.

She's no longer on her own. Doesn't have to fend for herself, find her own food, fight with other animals for shelter. Someone, something bigger and stronger, has picked her out.

But she also loses her freedom, her independence. Her ability to go off and roam in the woods, walk around the earth, stay out all night; create warm, loving, close communities with other wild animals, howl at the moon, pounce, run wild. She has somewhere she has to be. Someone she has to listen to. When he calls, she has to answer. She's bought and paid for, lock, stock and barrel. Domesticated/Domestic. What's the difference?

The tables turn. She goes from being the one who's taken care of, who is called, who is desired, who is the object of effort, to have her, to lure her into his vision of domestic bliss — to being the one who is doing the caring. Running the home. Taking care of him. Making sure he is fed, sometimes clothed. Stroking him, his body and his ego, to make him feel like he is the man he envisions himself to be. She takes care of him to make her life easier, yet she also has to take care of herself. Wash the dishes. Wash the clothes. The pretenses drop. She is no longer adored because he sees her without her make-up, without her fine lingerie, the always matching bra and panties. He sees the period panties, the raggedy ones that you don't mind getting bloody. No mystery, no allure, none of the wondering that keeps him coming back.

Regular. Average. Yes, even dowdy. In winter, it's flannel pajamas instead of bare skin. Creating one's own warmth, sheathing one's own body in heat becomes more important, more convenient, more normal than creating heat together.

The regular woman is the one who is taken advantage of. Taken for granted. Overlooked when she buys a new pair of glasses, changes her hair. He doesn't even notice. They get close, and they get further apart.

While dating, while wild, while undomesticated, he draws closer because he doesn't know and is trying to fathom her nature. But when married, given a ring as a symbol to keep others away, he feels that he knows her. At least well enough. At least enough so that the effort, that trying, is no longer required.

And she's happy to not try so hard too, lest I digress. It isn't easy to keep looking good, 24-7. High maintenance it is. Nails done, eyebrows waxed, makeup applied. She needs new clothes, new shoes to keep herself looking young and sexy so when he cheats on her, at least he'll come back. She's off to the hairdresser, regularly. When married, he gets to see what she has to do to keep her hair together. Or maybe he already knows. He does if he has sisters. And maybe he wants her to drop her pretenses. To be regular. To be herself. So he can see her and love her just as she is, without artifice. Maybe he thinks if he loves her this way, she will too.

11/26

I feel like the Energizer Bunny. I'm always running. From here to there. From chore to chore. It's endless. I do one and another beckons. I finish washing the dishes, and I have to do the floor. Sweep it, no time to mop it, because the laundry awaits. I have to fold what's in the dryer to move in a new load. I do that, and walk by the breakfast bar and see a stack of unpaid bills that I was going to get to when the kids said they were really hungry, so I had to mash the potatoes, move the turkey out of the pan to make the gravy, order them to get drinks for each other, and set the table, when what I really wanted to do was to have a second piece of cake and forget this so-called diet that I am on.

11/29

"…as if they had never been married." That's what the divorce decree I got in the mail today said. Over. Finished. Poof! Just like that. I'm free to marry as if I had never been married. Fourteen years and two kids later. A mirage. Smoke and mirrors, because that's how I pulled off every year after the third one when he first cheated on me. I made it look like a happy marriage, but now it's all for naught. Like it never existed. "As if they had never been married."

The work, the effort, the years, gone, with a stroke of the judge's pen. He sued me for divorce. He won. "As if they had never been married."

Eleven and a half years of being together, sleeping together, raising children. Over. How can you have and raise two kids and then, all of a sudden, it's "as if we had never been married." Are the kids a mirage? Or the residue? Are they what's left when the freedom to marry again is distributed, like the residue of an estate. The specific bequests are made, everything else is lumped into a category called the residue.

I gave myself up for the length of the marriage. I changed my personality. I let him use me, and now I am free to go forward "as if they had never been married." But what about reclaiming my lost self? That's not so easy. How do I get back those years when I was married to him? How do I act as if it's a mirage when the pain is so seared in my head that it's left a permanent burn mark, a keloid scar? How do I act as if I had never been married when it was the marriage that took my spirit, my energy, my self-confidence? If I act as if I had never been married, then what do I attribute the loss of myself to? My own efforts? A voluntary effort? Self-destructive tendencies?

No. It was a marriage that seemed like it was as phony and insignificant as the one that ended with the words "as if they had never been married." Like an annulment. Your life, your marriage: a legal fiction. No wonder people live together. You marry by saying, "I do," and what you do disappears with the words "as if they had never been married."

The decree itself was anticlimactic. The trial that resulted in it was hell, the true death of the marriage, as if two years of separation hadn't killed it in my heart already. In fact, it was dead long before that.

The decree means that I can legally retain my maiden name. Now, I guarantee that the name I got at birth is the one I will have at death. No wholesale changes. No hyphens. No more giving up of my basic identity to please someone else. No more being under anyone's thumb. I am free! An independent woman. I feel 21 again.

12/5

The feeling of peace is overwhelming. Trite, but true, it floods my body, the tension that seemed so much a natural, ever present part of me, the tension that had me running to the doctor for Prozac to ease it is gone. Gone after a night and a morning of good sex, no great sex; a pleasant evening with good dinner at an impressive, richly decorated, sensuous, Persian restaurant with equally impressive and fragrant food; a play, both of us dressed to impress the other; and a day unlike one I've had in ages. Eight hours of lying around Rick's sparsely furnished, yet modern, yet comfortable apartment, in soothing beige tones, on his comfortable couch, watching old movies on his 32" TV, taking mini-naps, closing my eyes when I felt like it, no responsibilities, lying in his arms, wrapping my arms and legs around him, he draping his arm over my shoulder, rubbing my baby soft hair that he loves with his strong, thick hands, kissing him, burying my head in his neck, caressing the little mound of hair left on his freshly cut hair. Being pleased. Taking in the pleasure. Languorous. A treat. Unusual. While I still feel him inside me, my skin throbbing where he entered me, my muscles wanting to wrap around something that is no longer there but that feels as real to me as if it were, the memory burned into my flesh, making me smile, wondering how long I can keep feeling this.

12/7

(Describing the time I just spent with Rick)

We lie on your couch, naked after making love, both not moving because we're tired, but also because, I suspect, if you feel as I do, we don't want to let go of each other. The apartment is warm from the heat that is turned up much warmer than I keep it at my big house and from the heat from making love when we both so desperately wanted each other to keep ourselves warm.

You enter me and push against me with all the fervor, passion, desire, yes, love, I think (yet it is too early to admit that) that has been bound up and held back by a marriage that has gone sour. I cling to you, press my fingers into your fleshy back, the muscles of your arms, your smooth, almost hairless legs, your buttocks, pulling you closer to me, trying to get you as far in me as you can go, as if that will erase the years of indifference I endured, the many times when I didn't want my husband to touch me but allowed it as a duty for which I got no credit and no pleasure. I try to get you to come in closer in me because, as you do, I feel you far up in my chest, between my breasts, touching parts of me that I didn't know existed for so long; thinking, or is it knowing, that sex with you would/could touch that part of me that would make me happy, feel valued, loved (even if you didn't say it), relaxed.

I snuggle my head against your arm, resting my head on your biceps, stroking your triceps with my hand. You wrap one arm around me, letting it rest somewhere between my breasts and my collar bone. Then you drape your other arm across my shoulder. Then you clasp our hands together, and sometimes you clasp my arm.

"I'm glad you came over tonight," you say. I thank you and say, "So am I."

You didn't have to say you were glad to have me there because I felt it as your grip tightened around me, felt it as you held me closer, wanting my warmth, pressing your nose into my hair and the back of my neck, stroking my skin with the tip of it, inhaling my perfume.

But I'm glad you said it. I feel that we have turned a corner. You call it "the no hassle test." I can come over, and it's no hassle for you. I can find my own food, my own drink. I know my way around enough to make things easy for you when I'm there.

I call it getting serious — of sorts. I know that my feelings have moved to another level, taken a leap to somewhere, I'm not quite sure where. I've crossed the line from thinking of you as someone I date to thinking of you as my boyfriend, even though that's not what you call yourself.

You love me as a lover, extol my praises, seems like you want me to stay. Making love with me almost made you cry, you said, it was so beautiful, and special and felt so good. I know that I touched something in you, too. As you thrust into me, it wasn't just about getting enough friction so you could explode, it was about giving yourself to someone who cared (I think); someone who still looked at you with wonder; someone who craved your touch, not cringed at it; someone you've never seen in curlers or ratty bath clothes; someone who sleeps naked with you, wanting nothing more than to feel your skin on hers, making sure that your bodies touched somewhere, in some way, when you slept; someone you've dreamed about; someone who looked to you to love her; someone who saw the good in you, who hadn't been hurt by you, or at least so hurt that she didn't care to repair the damage; someone who wasn't your wife. I think you felt like crying because you knew that when we made love that time, your soul was being poured in to mine, we were going somewhere that was much different, much more special than anywhere you've gone in a long time, the many times that you had sex with women you didn't care about for pure sex's sake. You knew that this was different and you almost cried because this was what you've always wanted. I know because I've always wanted it, too.

ﻉ

CHAPTER 22
I LONG FOR THE DAY WHEN IT'S NOT LIKE THIS

12/9, 11:31 p.m.

I PUT MY CHILDREN FIRST, but I resent it. As the wonderful tele-evangelist and Bible teacher Joyce Meyer says in her humorous, selfish, robot imitation, "What about me? What about me? What about me?"

Today I drove by the house that I didn't buy two months ago because my kids didn't like the small yard. The new owners had moved in. Just like that. Moved on with their lives, enjoying their house. While we waited. Stagnant. Because they didn't like the yard. Or was that an excuse. There was much about the house that I did not like, but this was the house that made me realize that I would not find a perfect house because I couldn't afford a perfect house.

Change of subject. But maybe not really.

I think I'm not ready for a relationship, and that makes me sad. I hold back the tears that are trying to get through. I'm good at holding them back, I hardly ever cry, so the tears stay welled up behind my eyes.

I passed on going out to a dinner/dance tonight with a girlfriend and her date, but without an escort for me, because I realized that I didn't need to go, preferred to put up my Christmas decorations, chill out with my kids, and put my house back in order after a week of having painters here. But I digress, because what I really want to record here is how much this relationship with Rick is hurting me. So, here's the story:

My girlfriend invited me to this dance, but me only. I couldn't bring an escort even though her selfish ass had a date, and my escort, of course, would have been Rick since he is the only man I'm seeing. So, I decided that I didn't want to go without him because the average age of the men in the group that sponsored the dance was about 60 and, although I liked older men, I didn't want to go that old. And, I realized how much I wanted to be with Rick. But I didn't think that Rick was available because a few days before today, he told me that his brother was coming up from Philly and that he was going to hang out with him tonight. Around 5 o'clock, I figured that the night was early, and that I could at least talk to Rick before he went out, at least hear his voice. So, like the needy, grasping woman-who-thinks-she's-in-love-or-at-least-deep-like that I am, I called him. And, guess what? He was free. His brother didn't come down. So now I'm pissed because he was free on a Saturday night and didn't call me. He didn't know that I had been thinking of going to that dance all week. As far as he knew, I was free that evening. So, even though I was again stung by the reality that he didn't care enough to call, didn't want to see me as much as I wanted to see him, I still thought it would be nice to spend the evening with him, even though *The Rules* and other books with advice for desperate women tell you not to accept an invitation extended on the same day. But when you have low self-esteem and some attention from a man is better than no attention from a man, you take what you can get.

But then I realized how complicated it would have been for me to spend the night with him because I had the kids, and I decided to accept my situation. Which was that on a Saturday night, I preferred to stay home with my kids rather than endure the hassle of going out. Even if I went over to Rick's, I still would have had to get the kids to my Mom's, bug them about packing their pajamas, packing their clothes for church, take 15 to 20 minutes to drive over to her house, drive back, and get up early in the morning to either take them to or meet them at church. I didn't want the hassle. Not even to be with someone who I truly wanted to be with, or did I? How much did I really want to be with him? Not so much that I would lose my pride and totally rearrange my life for someone who can't even call me when he's sitting home alone on a Saturday night.

I don't know. Now it seems like I'm chasing him, because even though I didn't go over, I called him and made the first move. I so don't want to fuck up this. Memories of Allen flood my head and how I fucked that up. Or did I? Rick says all the right things most of the time, and it's great to be with him, but I feel like I've crossed a line. I let him know that I want to be with him, that I care a great deal, and now I'm afraid he's going to run away and/or not reciprocate. He already doesn't call me or email me like he used to. I hear of other women I know who are sent flowers by the guys they're dating, and I'm not. I wonder if I'm making things too easy for Rick. I don't like the stage where I am. I feel myself retreating and hiding, hoping that he won't discover the "real" me because then he'd leave me. I have to maintain my self-confidence.

12/12

Today is the day I gave up. Gave in. Decided I couldn't do it on my own. That I had exhausted the limits of my mind, my will, my effort to keep myself up. To keep myself happy. To keep myself from drowning, falling in to the abyss that is constant, chronic, never-ending depression. Why can't I have my son's unbridled happiness? Because I'm not 11 years old, with someone else taking care of my needs, that's why.

So I ran out of energy to keep doing it myself and decided to take Prozac. Popped the first pill today. I look at it. Small and green. I was looking for magic.

I went to work and wondered if other people could tell. Would they see anything different?

12/13

Another land mine blew up today.

It's happened again. We've had what I've come to know as "The Talk". What is this relationship? Where is it headed? And he raised the issue. Unusual, so I should have known that it was bad news.

I feel like crying. I am holding back the tears. Every time I have one of these talks, I question whether I'm even ready to have a relationship, whether I'm emotionally stable enough to do it. The answer coming to me is no.

I didn't go to my son's school concert today. Couldn't sit through another one. Putting myself first or putting him off? I had a hectic day. Ran around, Christmas shopped, took Angela to the allergist in Boston — 45 minutes each way, raced home, had a few near-miss car accidents, was 40 minutes late for my counseling class, rushed in and did a practice counseling session that most of the other students in the class didn't understand, was criticized for it, came home waiting for Rick to call/come over/pick me up, because this is Wednesday and we always get together on Wednesday when the kids are with their father, and none of these things occurred. He says he's exhausted, worked hard, can't come over. Calls me from home instead of the office, like I thought he was going to.

Then, he asks me where I see things going, where I would like them to go, and I fall into the trap of answering him first. I say I see us spending time together, blah, blah, blah. He says as boyfriend/girlfriend? I say that'd be nice.

He says he's not ready for that. That he's still exhaling. I take that to mean that he's exhaling, present tense, with me. I guess when he's exhaled, past tense and past my use to him, he'll move on.

So, now I'm in the pull back mode. Pull back my feelings. Pull back planning my schedule around his, asking him to go to things with me. Trouble is, I like him, I like his company, I like his companionship. I like sex with him.

But I can't pull any of those things out of him, nor do I want to try to. It is insecurity that has me clutching, calling him, looking to him for things instead of sitting back and waiting, receiving. I've felt recently that he's taken me for granted, and now I understand why.

I am so sad. I long for the day when it's not like this. When someone loves me enough to want to be with me on a real, regular, predictable basis, when they care enough about me to call me everyday, to see how I'm doing, to want to see me in person, and not just for sex. I hope I get it. I'll wait for it.

12/13, 7 p.m. 2nd entry!

I don't think this Prozac is working. I still feel depressed. Nothing is coming to lift me away from the abyss. I feel myself falling over.

Maybe there's only so much depression Prozac can handle. Maybe even a drug can say — "enough already; what do you want, miracles?" Well, yes, as a matter of fact, I do. I don't want to feel bad anymore. Not another day. Not another second. I don't want to worry. I do want to be happy, as the song says.

I want to enjoy every moment, be happy that I have my health and strength, not to be grim about what I have or don't have or where I am or am not. I want to know that what **is** is what is supposed to be, and that it is all good.

I want to feel like I belong right where I am, not that my mission in life is to be somewhere else. I want to know that what I'm doing is what I should be doing. I want to feel comfortable in my own skin, in my own house, with my own furniture, with my life.

I do feel the Prozac kicking in a little bit. I do feel it saving me somewhat. I do feel competent to handle what comes my way even though I may not want it. I know that whatever pops up is not going to kill me or overwhelm me.

One thing I'm feeling is lonely and anxious. I'm lonely because I don't have a man who I can depend on fully, like I think I'd like to. I'm lonely because I didn't see my "boyfriend", if you can call him that, although he says that's not exactly how he sees things, although he wants to spend as much time as possible with me and screw my brains out, so I don't know what you can call him then; maybe a friend I screw or some guy I picked up off the street or at a friend's barbecue who I occasionally screw. Anyway, I didn't see him on Wednesday, our usual date night, so I'm lonely. I'm anxious because I'm not sure if I'm going to see him this weekend, if that will fit into his schedule or mine. I want to pin him down on it, but I can't. He won't be pinned down now. I'd like to see him tomorrow after the Christmas party I'm going to, but I'm not going to call him to push the issue any more. I'm going to leave it alone. I hope he'll raise the issue with me; I think he will, but I know I won't. I think one thing this Prozac is doing is stopping me from doing foolish things (or is that the normal, undepressed, high self-esteem thinking that this Prozac opens up?). Like, when I think of calling him, I feel paralysis washing over me. Something saying to me — no — don't do it. Don't go there. Don't even think of going there. So I don't. And am contented to do so.

ا.

CHAPTER 23

I FIGHT OFF THE FEAR THAT I REALLY AM FUCKED UP

12/14, 4:20 p.m.

TODAY I DECIDED TO GET MYSELF TOGETHER. Second day of Prozac. Thought like crying earlier today, but didn't; never do. That was before the Prozac kicked in. Now, when I feel depressive thoughts, I also feel myself coming back, being magically pulled back from the brink, the abyss.

But anyway, I decided to get myself together, fashion wise. I was drawn to those books at Barnes & Noble, drinking a gingerbread latte, which did not at all look like the frothy creation in the ad that tempted me to get that in the first place instead of a nice, strong, cup of regular coffee, or at least their Christmas Blend, which everybody else at the café but me seemed to know about.

I grabbed a cute book — *40 Things Every Woman Over 40 Should Know*. It was about changing your fashion look, staying current with your look, loving yourself enough to buy stuff that's not on sale, but only stuff that looks great on you, that you love. I'm going to go through my closet, get rid of the stuff that is more than five years old, stuff I no longer absolutely love. Stuff that doesn't make me feel great. She even wrote that a woman about to be divorced should get herself a good wardrobe full of things that she loves because she'll be feeling bad and that at least she'll be looking good on the outside. Same goes for post-divorce. I am going to clear out my closet, have only good quality, quirky things that make me feel great. I am worth it! She said repeat that over and over again until it is stuck in your head.

10:16 p.m.

The fear rises in my stomach like sea billows. It works its way up my chest, to my wind pipe before I summon the strength to stuff it down again. To grab it by the throat, the neck, the head, the ears, flip it over and pin it down. To stay down, to not rear its ugly head — I hope.

The fear is of many things. That I've made a mistake. That I'll never make the money my ex makes and that he will ever hereafter, forever, gloat that over me, buy the kids' affection, still seem like a good guy. If only they knew the incredible amount of hurt he put me through, a great deal of it intentional, they would be horrified, and in all likelihood, scarred for life. So I stuff that down, too. Pretend it never happened. Cast aside the hurt and disappointment and make dinner and breakfast and lunch, and then the next day, I do it all over again, hoping that they never go through what I did, nor inflict it on anyone, because, after all, they have his genes.

But I fight off the fear that I really am fucked up. That I really don't know how to have a good relationship. After the drama I had on the phone last night with my "boyfriend", after we had "The Talk", after that land mine blew up, he didn't call me today. No reaching out to reassure me. To see how I'm doing. To tell me how much he cares. That doesn't come, and for some strange reason, I take it pretty much as normal. Expected. I knew he didn't care that much; he's just showing it. I lived with, created the illusion that he really cared. Just me. Nobody else. Now that illusion is fading out, and I'm not surprised. I guess that's a mark of maturity.

I'm afraid that I'm not so talented, that I'll never be able to write a bestseller. Then what? That has been a dream of mine for so long, that has been who I am for so long, I don't know how to move on to anything else. I think I should start thinking about Plan B.

As I sit in this house, I wonder why, of course, I wonder why. I always wonder why. Why me? What did I do? I must have done something bad because where I am feels like punishment. It feels like growth and freedom, too, at times, but I guess that when I'm scared and worried it feels like punishment. I loved the wrong person the wrong way. What I got out of it was two great kids and a few hundred thousand dollars. Not bad really. Not bad for 11 years worth of work. But I missed a lifetime of happiness, fidelity, security, fun and love and sharing with one man. I wonder why I think I had to get it right the first time out? Why it hurts so bad that I didn't.

I don't want him. In fact, the sight of him now makes me sick, and I wonder why I ever did want him. I know I wanted the idea, I mourn the loss of that. I envy other women with marriages that look like they're happy. Women who can save their paychecks, buy what they want, go where they want, plan for a future with someone, and not work so hard.

It seems so hard to recreate that. Of course, when I'm really in a relationship with someone who wants that, it won't seem so hard. I'm always putting effort into something. I wonder when I'll be able to just stop and be and enjoy. I pray that it is soon.

12/18, 10 p.m.

Took the kids Christmas shopping so they could buy gifts for their friends. They are such good kids. I wonder at how we raised them. Two imperfect people, he more imperfect than me, of course, raised and raising two kind, loving, caring, intelligent, responsive children who love their parents. Maybe that's where our energy went. I know mine did. Into making sure that they weren't raised like I was, never having heard a parent, my mother, the only parent left after the untimely death of my father, say I love you until I was in college. And then I had to ask, so it didn't count.

My kids have heard "I love you" from both of us since they could hear. They say it, too, and are comfortable with it. I don't want them to fear saying it or hearing it.

Can't write anymore today. Too tense. My shoulders feel like they are pointing straight up, saluting, unnaturally, my effort going into keeping them tense, not relaxing.

12/22

Tonight I have my first free evening in a long time. I rented two videos, found one too juvenile, but thoroughly enjoyed the other. I revel in the silence. I've worked hard today, this year, and look forward to the next week off. No major responsibilities. Freedom.

Donald called (after I called him today to joke about whether he was going to invite me, a lifelong and avid Democrat to the inaugural ball that he was hosting for his candidate, George Bush, who stole the election), and Rick didn't call. I called Allen, too, and we had a nice friendly chat. He propositioned me at the end. I wonder if he really meant it. I should call his bluff, or, I wonder if he is calling mine. If he comes over, will I really make love to him?

I've always considered myself a one woman man, and that man is Rick now, but I don't want him to take me for granted I don't feel that he's fully committed to me. So if he's not, why should I be? Why should I sit around waiting for him? I should be going out. It's kind of like I have to force myself to do that, but so be it. I don't want to sit around and wait if I do in fact want to be with someone. This Christmas break, when he goes home for the holidays, will tell me how much he misses me. We'll see whether and how often he calls, what he says, what he does when he returns next Wednesday, after Christmas, after he would have gone 10 days without seeing me — a long time for us. We'll see what I do, too.

12/23

What a wonderful evening. Had dinner with Barbara and Janice, two women who are also single mothers not by choice. Strong. Carrying on despite the situation that they find themselves in. One not of their design, not of their liking, not always, not what they expected. Yet they endure. They go on. They raise their daughters and their sons, even without the help that I get when Dad comes to pick up the kids because their kids' Dads are not around.

We strengthen each other. We band together. We understand each other. Our children understand each other, too. Each is dealing with loss, the absence of a "normal" family, yet finding that what is normal depends. Finding normalcy with each other. Strengthening each other like the mothers strengthen each other.

We'll never know everything our children are thinking. But, as we sit around the dining room table, talking about what it's like dating and having sex with men after being with one man for 10, 11, 15 years, I wonder if the kids sit around talking about how it hurts not to have a father.

I identify with the poor wounded children who've lost their father, because that is me. Abandoned. Always wondering what might have happened had he lived.

We had to reconstitute our worlds. A world without husbands and fathers or at least live-in fathers. Had to/have to create a world that works for us and our children. It's different. It's not what we bargained for. But that doesn't mean that it can't be good.

ॐ

CHAPTER 24
TAKE THE TIME, CONCENTRATE, AND STOP THE PAIN

12/24, 11:24

MY BOYFRIEND WOULD HAVE CALLED BY NOW. Two days and no contact. One week since I've seen him. It is the holidays and everyone's feeling more sentimental — me included. I was missing him a lot earlier, under the illusion/delusion that he cared/missed me, too.

I don't dare call him as he's down with his family, and I don't want to interrupt. Don't want to pry. Don't want him to feel like I'm tracking him down. But I miss him. I think he knows that. I think he knows that I won't call, but that I want him to.

11:51 p.m.

Went to church today. A nice service reminding us to look back on the blessings of this year and look ahead for more. I think of the incredible year I had and how I made it.

Came home, wrapped presents, took a nap. Put off baking Christmas cookies until tomorrow. We were all too tired. Rented a cute video about people finding each other.

Still no phone call from Rick. Out of sight, out of mind? I worry that he's ensconced in family life, loves it, misses it, and decides that our relationship, such as it is, is over. But then I think that can't be. All I know is I want more than I have now. So, I have to pray for what I want and take steps to get it.

12/26

The day after Christmas. The first day of Kwanzaa. The day before Rick comes back or is it the day he comes back? I don't know because he didn't tell me exactly. I just know that he'll be back tomorrow. And I hope to see him.

I'm torn between asking him why he went for four days without calling me, but I know why. I'm tempted to ask him if he slept with his wife, but what would I do with the answer? I'm tempted to raise the issue of New Year's Eve, but I want him to raise it first.

I would have liked some real, solid evidence that he cares (a call). Truth is I miss him and wish he cared enough to call. I hate that I'm waiting around for him to do so.

I feel that I need to see other people, keep myself occupied, not fall for him like it appears I have. It seems like he's fallen for me, too. He acts it, but he says something different. If I really believe what he says, I'll start seeing others. The thing is — how do I stop caring? This has always been hard for me. I don't know how to be nonchalant, especially after I've let someone into my heart. How do I pull him out, extract him like a splinter, because that's what he's like, he hurts a little bit but it's a pain that can be endured for a while. But then after a while, it becomes irritating, the pain dull, but enough of a constant reminder that you have to do something about it. So one day, you pull it out, take the time, concentrate, and stop the pain. The small scar, the point where it entered your body, heals, new skin grows, and you go on, forgetting that it was even there.

I'd like to get to that point if I don't get to the point where he acknowledges that he loves me, that I'm his girlfriend, that he's my boyfriend, and that things are cool, that I'm comfortable and can relax in a nice relationship. I want it. I deserve it, and I'm going to have it. If not with him, with someone. I have a lot to give.

11:15 p.m.

I laid in my bed, my son sick beside me, thinking that I was forgotten, and Rick called.

12/28

The feeling I feel now is contentment. Physically. Mentally. Physically, Rick made love to me with such intensity and desire yesterday that I can't imagine how it feels to receive someone who wants me more. He gave me orgasms so intense, his tongue dancing, light, strong, pushing, licking, sucking, moving around, not letting me pull back, giving me pleasure in mini-orgasm after mini-orgasm. I knew it was going to be good. When he started, I just laid back and purred.

He snuck in again around 6 a.m., both of us still lying down, him stirring me up, and him squealing, moaning, crying out with delight. I wonder if it's because of the heat, the sound, the feel, or just that it's me. Whatever it is, I loved it and wanted to tell him so, but we're not there yet.

My mental contentment comes from the fact that he missed me and said so, didn't sleep with his wife, talked to me about his life, and feelings and experiences, and, as he talked, I found myself so drawn to him, my feelings so intense, I knew I was falling in love but couldn't say it yet.

12/30

It's a snowy, blizzard-like day. At 6:10 p.m., I'm snowed in and alone. But I am satisfied beyond measure. I don't think I have ever felt so satisfied.

Rick came over last night and left me this morning, totally and thoroughly sexually satisfied. And what that has done for me (alone or in combination with the Prozac) has left me grounded, totally satisfied and comfortable in my skin.

There is not a drop of strain or stress in my body. I don't feel l like I need to be anywhere or do anything. I'm fully present and comfortable.

Last night he woke me up again in the middle of the night, as he is wont to do. That now familiar feeling of him pushing up behind me, pulling at me, trying to find a way in. He lifts my left leg ever so slightly. I shift my body to the right to nestle in and get comfortable and find the right angle for him. I hold his leg, lay it between my breasts, wrap my hand around the muscles in his forearm and settle in as he pushes in and out, up and down. But this time it's different; he wants to go in deeper. He changes position. He moves sideways. I wonder if the intensity and variety of his lovemaking signals his deeper feelings for me. I suspect that it does. I hope that it does.

I move against him differently, too. Not just up and down, in and out, but side to side and up and down in waves, pushing myself urgently against him, wanting to hear him scream my name, or moan, or purr, or curse, or express the deep pleasure that I know I am giving him. And he does. And I do. And when he comes, we both are exhausted and amazed with the variety of sex that we have and how good it is. He said that I screwed his brains out. It's been a while since I've heard that, or maybe I never had. But when he was finished, I wanted to tell him that now I know what it's like to be truly screwed, but I didn't. Later I called him and told him that I was basking in the glow of total sexual satisfaction.

And I was. And I wonder if I would have been much happier these past 14 years if I was getting great sex, sex like that on a regular basis, and I figured that I would have been, and that made me sad. But now I know that it is possible to be totally satisfied, totally relaxed, fully present, feeling loved, and that all is right with the world.

I didn't have it before, but I won't do without it again.

(Undated Entry)

Rick and I talked about making our fortunes by working together on a book.

Book Idea:

— How to Care for a Dog... The Two-Legged Variety

— The Dog Trainer's Guide to Keeping/Caring for a Man (the principles are the same)

— The Dog Owner's Guide to Caring for a Man

— If You Can Take Care of a Dog, You Can Take Care of a Man

— Dogs and Men: Common Principles for their Care and Feeding

— Common Principles...

— The Care and Feeding of Dogs and Men

ào

12/31, 11:57

BOOM! Another land mine.

And I really didn't see that one coming. New Years Eve, and I thought I'd spend it with Rick. End the year wrapped up in his arms, start the new year off making love, excited about the future. Him content with me, and me content with him.

But, that's not what's happening. He still hasn't made up his mind about what he 's doing tonight, he says. He may want to go out with his friends. (Of course, if it was just with his male friends, there'd be no reason why I couldn't go with him, for who doesn't want a date on New Year's Eve?) It just hit me that he may be going out with another woman. That he's waiting to hear from her. That I'm someone he can screw and see when he wants to, but not someone he has to plan for. That it's preferable to hang out with the guys, if that's what he's doing, to being with me. That this is huge.

I've sat around waiting for him to call, waiting for him to decide that he wants to be with me as much as I want to be with him. But, it's not true. Even after the wonderful time we had yesterday. Even how he said that this relationship was going to last for a while. Now, I feel like a fool. A used fool. A convenient fool. A hurt fool.

Of course, I wonder why I put up with this shit. Why I didn't tell him on the phone to go screw himself, that he had hurt me beyond repair, but I suspect that he knew that and didn't care. What was I afraid of? That he wouldn't want me anymore? Well, he acted like that already. I asked him to say yes or no, and he said maybe. I put it bluntly — so, if something better comes along, you'll do that, otherwise, you'd like to be with me. Plan B. Second choice. He said right.

A year of dating, a lifetime of dating, and I still don't have it right. Still have put myself in a position to be hurt, taken advantage of. How could I be so dumb?

I should stay home tonight and assess where I've been, what I've done this year, what I've done right, what I've done wrong. Just when I think I have it figured out, I don't. Another bomb dropped. Another land mine explodes, and I am maimed, injured. Another piece of shrapnel under my skin, staying there, festering, unable to be removed, irritating me, drawing pus to it, creating pus, and poisoning me.

I'm sick of this shit. This year, I want to declare my independence. But I want love. I want sex. I want someone to be there for me. To respect me. To be kind to me. I don't know how that's going to happen. I just know that eventually it will. When the time is right. When God decides. In the meantime, I'll keep walking through life, aware that the land mines are out there, stepping as gingerly as I can, but staying in the game, not hiding from life nor love, realizing that it can all blow up, a land mine can go off, but that I can go back into my hospital, be treated and released, live with the scars, yet not let them stop my spirit from going on, from carrying on, from being all that I can be and then some.

☉

2:45 p.m.

I need a better metal detector. 45 years old and I still can't see the land mines. They're buried under layers of sand, silt, deception, lies, and I don't know they're there. I need a metal detector that goes off at the slightest clue. A very sensitive one. As sensitive as I am. Sensitive to the presence of someone who doesn't care or doesn't care as much as I do. I need lights flashing, bells ringing, warnings buzzing in my ear, telling me to avoid this one, don't get too close to that one, look out, the danger here is powerful, go that way, go this way, walk around this one and don't go back.

In my single/pre-married days, I never had a good detector that helped me avoid the worse of and in men, but when I saw the worse, I walked away. Not without getting hurt, because I got that. But I generally didn't give a second thought to walking away.

Third entry today — 6 p.m. — this is really, really bad

Laid back in my chair, head thrown back, listening to Phyllis Hyman's "Living in Confusion", about a man who did her wrong, led her on, and then "I Don't Want to Lose You," about a woman/man trying to hold on to a confused lover. Tears just about to fall, stomach churning like butter, throat sore and tight, tension shortening the muscles. Another love TKO-ed.

My therapist said don't feel stupid if it's something you couldn't have known. I think that I should have known. Should have seen the signs. I was lulled into thinking they weren't there. Let down my guard. Believed what he said. He said, "I miss you," and I believed it. He said "This relationship will last for a while," and I believed him; I wanted to. He refers to himself as "my man", and I think — I'm glad he feels that way.

Then he doesn't see me on New Year's Eve. Makes other plans when he knows I'm waiting on him. Takes me for granted. Hurts me.

I think — what a fool I've been. I've screwed him, made love to him, exposed myself to him in a most basic way, in a way that really means something to me, and he throws that away, looks at that casually, puts me in my place. I guess he looks at it casually because it is casual sex. But I recall all that talk about him being my next long-term relationship and me making the right decision as far as he is concerned, which is my deciding to date and have sex with him. Now I feel like we need to go back to just being friends, to take sex out of the equation until there's a serious commitment, until he can appreciate the gift I've given him, until he can treat me with the respect I deserve, not like some hoochie momma whore or something. If he goes out and screws someone tonight (why do I write "if" when I know the word is "when"), that's the end of him having sex with me. So, I guess that's it. It makes me sad to think of that, because the sex was so enjoyable, but that's the way it's going to be.

I respect myself and respect myself more than he apparently does. I really do want commitment and fidelity. It may be a naive notion, but I guess I'm just naive. I try to think the best of others and that they could be like I am. Maybe that's stupid, but I don't want to be a bitch or to have a hard heart. I'm not that kind of person. I don't want my essential nature to change because of someone else.

But I sure feel like I have put my trust in the wrong person. Have been blind sided, have been led down a path and then beaten over the head.

And now I feel embarrassed. I have to explain why there will be no Rick to my kids. Have to have them see the reality of a failed relationship. They wanted to meet him but, sorry, the relationship is over before they get that chance.

But maybe that's OK. OK that they know that sometimes things don't work out. But, as children of divorce, they know that already.

Maybe it's OK that they know that Mom's not perfect, that she can have failed relationships — but they know that already.

Maybe it's OK that they know that Mom is fucked up — but they know that already, too. I know that. It feels like the whole world knows that.

I'm tired of being hurt. Tired of putting my heart out there. Tired of hoping and waiting, watching, thinking he'll change his mind, see the error of his ways, see how special I am.

I guess I have to be tough. When I decided to keep seeing Rick a few months ago, I decided that I wasn't going to be bound by my fears, that I was going to just judge him on what happened between me and him.

Treat me with kindness and respect, I told him, and we'll get along fine. Today, I got neither. And, I got disrespected in a big way. So, based on that, I need to end it, to change the relationship, to not be so exposed, so vulnerable, to take the sex out, to not be so bare, so naked with my feelings. So I'll keep my clothes on. It's symbolic, really. My clothes are a symbol of my feelings. Every layer of clothes is a layer of my feelings that I don't reveal. Every layer of clothes hides something — my heart, my love, my spirit. When I'm fully clothed, no man can get it all. I can't take the risk of exposing myself to you. Naked and bare, I expose my feelings and my heart. You are close to my heart, you can see it beating. I'm vulnerable, unprotected, trusting. But now, I'm pulling back to be fully clothed. I'm pulling back; the walls are going back up. The shell is growing. The guard, the fortress, the moat. I've been hurt, and I'm hiding inside. Who will be able to pull me out?

ði

1/1

LAST NIGHT I WROTE "Who will be able to pull me out?" Forget that — I'm pulling myself out. Enough of the pity party. It's amazing what daylight and a new year can do. A blank slate. A fresh start. I've taken enough shit, and I'm not taking any more. At least not this year. I'm going to sell my house, buy a new one, find a new man — or better yet, let him find me, and tell everyone who doesn't support me to take a flying leap. I'm not spending any more time crying about someone who doesn't care about me and who shows it. This year, it's all about me. Full speed ahead. Damn the torpedoes.

I'll never have another night like last one. Man or no man. I'll never end the year feeling rejected and down. I'll look back on all that I have accomplished, pat myself on the back for making it through another year, and work my plan for the new year. I promise. Wait — is that a New Year's Resolution? I know how easy they are to break. So, even though I'm resolving to do better this new year, henceforth and forever more, this is not a New Year's resolution. This is a new me.

THE END

This section is about telling your own story.

No one has to read it but you, but telling your story — or at least bits and pieces of it — on paper is important. If you're like Carolyn and all of the other people, fictional or real, who journal through personal life challenges, you'll find it to be therapeutic.

There are a lot of thoughts in your head. There are a lot of feelings in your heart. You have a lot of decisions to make, many for the first time. You may feel like a lot is riding on each decision you make — because it is. It's your life. And, if you have children, it's their life, too.

Most everyone's familiar with that old advice of writing down the pros and cons of something when you need to make a decision. Sometimes it's more complex than that. During your separation and divorce, there will be so many thoughts moving through your head in a jumble that you'll feel overwhelmed. You'll look for some help to unscramble them.

Like Carolyn, writing down your thoughts might help you make sense of them. Putting them on paper will get them out of your head — sometimes permanently, and sometimes just for a blessed, little while. Maybe, like Carolyn, you won't write at all for a long period of time. Her situation seemed too overwhelming, too bad, too crazy, too illogical, too much to deal with. That's ok, too. Sometimes you won't feel like writing, but, other times, you'll need that therapeutic experience.

So, this section of the book is about journaling. Use a journal, a notebook, or just grab a few sheets of paper. But grab something that you can use to record your thoughts as they come to you. At anytime. At any date.

Most of you, most of the time, won't need any prompts to tell your story — it will just flow out of you. Just tell it. Just write it. Validate yourself. Make sense of the confusion. Work it out.

But, if you need prompts or want prompts, there are prompts that cover situations that you will likely encounter and questions that can help you address the issues floating around in your soul.

You don't have to share your story or your feelings with others, but you may want to. You can share in a counseling support group that you're already in, or you can create one.

With that, tell your story. Don't let separation or divorce silence you. Even if you're the only one listening to what you have to say, that's enough.

— Peace,

Sheilah Vance

Pick a prompt and write what you feel. There's no right or wrong. There's only you.

1) When I realized my marriage was ending...

2) When I realized my marriage was over...

3) When my spouse moved out...

4) When I moved out...

5) When I/we told the children we were separating...

6) When I found out my spouse was having an affair...

7) When I realized my financial situation...

8) When I started looking for a lawyer...

9) When I found a lawyer...

10) My first meeting at the lawyer's office...

11) When I was served with divorce/child support/spousal support papers...

12) When I filed for divorce...

13) When I filed for child support...

14) When I filed for alimony...

15) When I had to move out of my house...

16) When I had to sell my house...

17) When I received my first support check...

18) When I realized how little I was going to receive for child support/spousal support/alimony...

19) When I realized how much I had to pay for child support/spousal support/alimony...

20) When the house was sold...

21) When I went to counseling...

22) When my spouse went to counseling...

23) When we went to couples counseling...

24) When my children went to counseling...

25) My children started acting up when...

26) I started acting up when...

27) My spouse started acting up when...

28) Putting the children to bed...

29) Going to bed alone...

30) Going to bed with someone new...

31) The first time I had sex after my separation/divorce...

32) Sex...

33) Love...

34) The fairy tale...

35) When I told people about my separation/divorce...

36) When people found out about my separation/divorce...

37) The divorce disease...

38) My energy level...

39) My wedding ring...

40) My children's school work...

41) My children's teachers....

42) My children's friends...

43) I don't trust myself because...

44) I trust myself because...

45) My self-esteem...

46) When I saw the divorce decree...

47) My support hearing/conference...

48) When I saw our separation agreement...

49) My spouse's new girlfriend/boyfriend...

50) It's not fair...

51) Fairness...

52) I feel so sad when...

53) I feel so happy when...

54) I feel so accomplished when ...

55) My mother...

56) My father...

57) The other members of our family...

58) Our friends...

59) My church family...

60) My church...

61) My pastor...

62) Other women...

63) My women's group...

64) When I realized I had to get a job...

65) My job...

66) My boss...

67) My coworkers...

68) My car...

69) Exercise...

70) I feel so tired when...

71) Fatigue...

72) Energy...

73) Sleep...

74) Men...

75) Women...

76) Disappointment...

77) Joy...

PRESENTATIONS

SHEILAH VANCE, ESQ. is available for workshops, motivational speaking, continuing legal education, and book signings on issues related to separation, divorce, dating again, reinventing yourself, and living your dreams. Some of Vance's most popular presentations include:

- The Top 10 Land Mines of Divorce
- 10 Things Every Married Woman Should Know
- Divorce from the Client's Perspective
- Reinventing Yourself
- How to Chase Your Dreams and Make Them Come True
- How to Write and Publish Your Book

For more information about Sheilah's presentations, books, The Elevator Group and all of its authors, visit www.TheElevatorGroup.com or email info@TheElevatorGroup.com.

ELEVATOR GROUP
· PUBLISHING ·
Helping People Rise Above™

PO Box 207, Paoli, PA 19301
610-296-4966
www.TheElevatorGroup.com
info@TheElevatorGroup.com

Also available from The Elevator Group:

- *Journaling Through the Land Mines*, by Sheilah Vance. A companion journal to Land Mines. 200 pages. Includes the 77 *"Journaling Through the Land Mines"* journaling prompts from the Reader's Guide in *Land Mines* and plenty of blank pages sprinkled with inspirational quotes to help you journal through your own land mines.
- *Chasing the 400*, a novel, by Sheilah Vance.

Also available from The Elevator Group Faith:

- *A Christian Woman's Journal to Weight Loss*, by Patricia Thomas.
- *A Christian Woman's Journal to Weight Loss Affirmation Cards*, by Patricia Thomas.

Coming in summer 2009 from The Elevator Group Faith:

- *Creativity for Christians: How to Write your Story and Stories of Overcoming from the Members of One Special Church*, by Sheilah Vance with Rev. Felicia Howard. We are made overcomers by the blood of the lamb and the word of our testimony (Rev. 12:11). Everyone has a story to tell. Learn how to tell yours. 50% writing workshop. 50% stories of victory. 100% inspiring.

For more information about any of the items above, visit
www.TheElevatorGroup.com.
To order any of the items above, contact
Atlas Books Distribution
30 Amberwood Parkway
Ashland, Ohio 44805
or place your order toll-free at 1-800-247-6553
or on-line at www.atlasbooks.com.

ELEVATOR GROUP
* PUBLISHING *

Helping People Rise Above™